"Rebekah Bergman's exploration of our strange biologies reads like the irresistible beating hands of time. This daughter of Mary Shelley delights and excites the border between story and science as she doles out questions that both haunt and expose our obsessions."

—**SAMANTHA HUNT**,
author of *The Unwritten Book*

"In *The Museum of Human History*, Rebekah Bergman offers readers what we as individuals can rarely see on our own: the interconnectedness that hums between every human being, the high cost of painlessness and hard truths of our inevitable obsolesce. This is a novel about what we want and also what we can't escape—a story as heartbreaking as it is seductive."

—**ALLEGRA HYDE**,
author of *Eleutheria*

"There are no static exhibits or neatly segmented timelines in Bergman's *The Museum of Human History*. Here, lives bleed into each other, echoing on decades, centuries, millennia after they end (if they end). A haunting chord of a novel that will hang in the air long after you turn the final page."

—**TIFFANY TSAO**,
author of *The Majesties*

"Rebekah Bergman's *The Museum of Human History* is one of the most agile novels I have read in a long time. It reads like a documentary retold as a dream retold as a mystery novel. What a wise, good-hearted debut!"

—**KATE BERNHEIMER**,
author of *Fairy Tale Architecture*

The Museum of Human History

The Museum of Human History

A NOVEL

REBEKAH BERGMAN

TIN HOUSE / PORTLAND, OREGON

This is a work of fiction. All of the characters, organizations, and events portrayed in this novel are either products of the author's imagination or are used fictitiously.

First US Edition 2023
Printed in the United States of America

Manufacturing by Sheridan
Interior design by Beth Steidle

Library of Congress Cataloging-in-Publication Data

Names: Bergman, Rebekah, 1989– author.
Title: The museum of human history : a novel / Rebekah Bergman.
Description: Portland, Oregon : Tin House, [2023]
Identifiers: LCCN 2023005441 | ISBN 9781953534910 (paperback) | ISBN 9781953534996 (ebook)
Subjects: LCGFT: Science fiction. | Novels.
Classification: LCC PS3602.E75565 M87 2023 | DDC 813/.6—dc23/eng/20230210
LC record available at https://lccn.loc.gov/2023005441

Tin House
2617 NW Thurman Street, Portland, OR 97210
www.tinhouse.com

DISTRIBUTED BY W. W. NORTON & COMPANY

1 2 3 4 5 6 7 8 9 0

For Penina

The horses fell asleep in their stalls, the dogs in the courtyard, the pigeons on the roof, the flies on the walls, and even the fire on the hearth flickered, stopped moving, and fell asleep. The roast stopped sizzling. The cook, who was about to pull the kitchen boy's hair for having done something wrong, let him loose and fell asleep. The wind stopped blowing, and outside the castle not a leaf was stirring in the trees.

"LITTLE BRIER-ROSE"
THE BROTHERS GRIMM

The Museum of Human History

PART ONE

–1–

A QUARTER CENTURY OF SLEEP

THE GROUND IS NOT YET SHAKING, AND THE CAVES ARE solid and unmoving as the doors of the Marks Museum of Human History open and the audience files in.

Seats are found in the central hall. Coats are placed on chair-backs. Programs are picked up and paged through. Throats are cleared.

The air is damp and musty and holds the scent of sweat and impending rain. Old neighbors from Jacob's Circle gesture with chins to avoid pointing as they whisper, "Look—there's the father."

The father smiles his goofy, sad smile at no one. He appears the same, if older.

Beside the father, there is a woman with vacant brown eyes that dart around. She holds the arm of a man with a very serious expression and perfect posture. The two strangers and the father make their way to three empty chairs at the front of the room. The man holds a hand to the father's back. This, presumably, is to support him, though it is also a gesture not unlike a puppet master's.

In the aisles, the former Congregants reunite and greet one another. Their traditional orange robes are faded from too many washings. They say hello and hug, but their eyes are fixed on the caves before them.

They have been waiting for this for a long time.

Inside the caves, once, there were the remains of prehistoric humans. Inside the caves, now, there is Maeve Wilhelm.

Maeve has been sleeping, breathing, and not aging for twenty-five years.

At the front of the line, a large man in a gray suit pushes through to find a seat with an unobstructed view.

And outside, a woman driving a rental car pulls into the parking lot. She's going to be late, she knows. She holds a stone in her fist and reminds herself what she has come here to do.

–2–

Ten years before Maeve's sleep

THE MAN WAS SHORT WITH A SAD-LOOKING MUSTACHE, but a mustache was not a permanent feature, so the singles event at the bar where Naomi Clarke met her future widower was not as bad as she had feared it would be. The songs were playing at a reasonable volume. She could hear him over the music, but she could use the music as a topic of conversation if they began floundering.

She asked the mustached man what he did for work, realizing a half second later, with some dread, that this question was bound to bounce back at her. He was telling her of Curious Critters, the insect and arachnid museum he had recently opened. It was in the shopping center next to the hair salon right off the exit to Marks Island City. The storefront that still looked like a deli, did she know it?

No, she couldn't say that she did.

"I have to work on our marketing," he said, undeterred. "People keep coming in wanting an exterminator."

Was that a joke? She could not decide. She looked at him quizzically.

So, she thought, an entomologist. That could be endearing. Couldn't it? Science would be something they had in common.

Both of their fields branched off from biology. There was that at the very least: life.

He did begin to tell jokes now. Bad jokes. Not distasteful, just bad. Entomology puns. Why didn't the butterfly go to the prom? She heard it was a moth ball. That kind of thing.

If she forced a laugh, Naomi knew it would sound fake, so she did not laugh. Instead, she arranged her face to gesture toward laughing. She squinted and tilted her head back at an angle and blew a little air out her nose in a barely audible huff. This was enough to keep him going. How many insect puns might one man know? Quite a few, it turned out.

She tried not to look at the bald spot emerging at the top of his head. She pretended she could not see this dry patch of scalp as she stood at the bar beside him. She had a bird's-eye view and though she tried not to think this, it *did* look like an egg resting inside a wispy-thin nest.

Stop, she told herself. She dug her nails into her palms. She could be happy if she decided to be.

This was a sentence she liked to repeat. She did not think it was true, but she liked pretending she was the type of person who could trust in something that simple: that you could be happy if you decided to bc. Magic.

Finally, the man fell silent.

"And how about you?" he asked, as she'd known he would. "What do you do?"

Lionel was marveling at the woman as he rattled off bug puns. He would soon exhaust his inventory, which she seemed to delight in. She had long legs and a beautiful globe of curls. The scalp of his own bald spot reddened, hotly, but he tried to take faith in his mustache. Without meaning to, he twitched his nose so that his mustache writhed.

He had never been to a singles event. He came to this one prompted by a recent milestone in his nascent adulthood: the opening of his insect museum.

Lionel's father, a physician and entrepreneur, had hoped his son would become a different kind of scientist. But when Lionel chose bugs, his father had loaned him the money to get the museum up and running with no expectation that he'd be repaid. Lionel was not entirely self-unaware. He knew his father lacked faith in him. But he was also relentlessly optimistic, about his newest endeavor as with most aspects of his life. He'd had no reason not to be; good things had happened and so they could keep on happening.

When he pictured the future, Lionel saw himself as he hoped he would be. That was, presenting tarantulas to squeamish six-year-olds, pinning perhaps his hundredth exotic butterfly to the exotic butterfly wall, turning his passion into a living. How lucky he was.

But while he loved his critters, he was mostly convinced that they did not love him back and never would. He did not blame them for this. They were incapable. But he did not want to be—in that future he was certain he'd grow into—alone with his unrequited bug love. What he needed, he had thought, pleased with his knack for wordplay, was a lovebug.

He'd lost the thread of what the woman was saying. He had been too preoccupied by her legs and her hair and his own reminiscing, and—anyway—what did she do for work? He had just asked her that. Damn. It was some kind of scientist. Right?

"So, where is your office?" he asked, he hoped, casually.

"Downtown. You know, the Genesix facility?"

Biotech, that was it!

Genesix Labs was one of the three biotech companies that had recently built outposts in the city. None had publicly shared what they were developing. How exciting. A brilliant and beautiful woman of science and intrigue.

It was surprising too, this new position. She went on to tell Lionel that she had not been expecting the job offer. Biotech, she explained, was not her field of study.

"No?" he said.

No, her doctorate was in paleobiology.

"That's a funny change," Lionel acknowledged. He knew nothing of paleobiology and, honestly, he wasn't very interested. Paleoentomology, maybe. But even then. Insects were old and relatively unchanging and that was partly what he loved about them.

He could tell that she took pride in her studies. It was obvious from how she'd said the word "doctorate."

"Did you study Marks Island?" Marks Island proper was not an actual island. It was connected to the city by an isthmus. But thousands and thousands of years ago, it really was an island. Everyone knew at least this much local history: Marks Island had been home to humans far earlier than any humans were thought to have lived anywhere else in this part of the world.

"It was the focus of my research," she said.

"The ancient tribe?"

"Well, the whole ancient ecosystem," she said, "but I won't bore you." She looked at him. "Not yet."

"I wasn't always a bug guy myself," Lionel said. "My first love was astrophysics. It's strange sometimes, the paths life takes us to."

Before Lionel learned to see the universe in an anthill, he'd seen the universe solely in the universe itself. His father had harbored great hopes for his only child becoming an astronaut. But in the end, while Lionel enjoyed the abstract parts—the puzzles and thought experiments presented by the fabric of spacetime—any concrete consideration of the cosmos overwhelmed him. More than once he had hyperventilated during a lecture to the point of nearly passing out. He couldn't bear how small he was. Infinitesimal. That was the word for it. He shifted to insects. They had their own tiny cosmos where he was a god.

If Lionel were a more perceptive man, he might have seen that, unlike him, this woman had not found a more stable, deeper love in the career she'd unexpectedly stumbled into.

All her life, Naomi had been pulled by her single scholarly pursuit, which she had followed ferociously: the reconstruction of ancient systems of life. For her dissertation, she was given permission by the Marks Foundation to excavate on their shores. There were still many mysteries about the former island. Naomi had been hoping to solve some.

She'd developed a theoretical model of the ecosystem and she had published a paper. The research made waves in academic circles, so she'd assumed she would be able to secure a postdoctorate. After defending her thesis, she was awarded the top prize from the Academy of Paleobiologists in a ceremony she'd had actual dreams about.

But as she heard herself introduced and as she stepped forward to accept the award from the president of the academy, she knew it was the end of that dream.

The funding landscape had shifted during her years of graduate school, leaving no space for the ancient sciences. There were no grants that would allow her to continue the research she'd been digging into—literally digging into—for years. In what felt like a final bit of symbolism, the Marks Foundation closed Grace Beach, where she'd been excavating, to the public.

She'd never dig out there again, she realized. The disappointment of this felt starkly familiar.

In high school and into college, Naomi had been an open-water swimmer. She had been one of the fastest in the division, though she had quit the sport to take her first coveted work-study job at the lab.

As she accepted the award at the academy, she was reminded of what it had felt like to swim those long races. Concentrating on the distance she had to travel, committing to that expanse of ocean, pushing her body beyond what she thought her body or any body was capable of, and, at the end, looking up to see two things simultaneously: that she'd won and that she was alone.

True success came with loneliness. She had known this before and now she knew it again.

The three new biotech outposts had been all that her classmates wanted to talk about during their final months of graduate school. It was either that or continue lamenting the lack of jobs and their pitiful, overeducated predicaments. Their conversations were tinged with resentment and skepticism. The rumored political ties to "Big Bio" and the "looming crisis of bioethics" they felt the city—the world—would soon be thrust into. Naomi found this chatter excessively dramatic but not altogether baseless. There *was* that billionaire biotech mogul, and his electoral influence was well documented.

Two days after the awards ceremony, a man from Genesix showed up outside her lab. He looked like a comic book villain—slick hair combed back from his wide forehead, an expensive suit, a dimpled chin, prominent eyebrows. In his enormous hands, he held a copy of her CV.

He introduced himself as Dr. Gregory Dean. He said he had heard of Naomi and of her work. That he was impressed by it, and by her commitment to science, and why didn't she leave the ancient past now and join his team in designing the future? It felt like a pickup line.

Plus, he said, the pay would be tremendous. When he smiled, his skin tightened in a way that made Naomi consider the shape of his skull.

"Let me sleep on it," she said.

His smile snapped closed in an instant. "Sleep," he told her, like a command.

But he didn't move and she felt she couldn't either. He had one more thing to say. Life advice from a biotech executive. "Naomi," he said, his voice changing completely, "you know, you can be happy if you decide to be."

She reconsidered him at that moment. Was he an idiot? He couldn't really believe that. Could he?

Then again, it was a nice idea. Simple. And anyway, she didn't really need to sleep on her decision. There were no other offers, so she took the job.

What did it say about her that she hadn't told a single classmate that she'd be working for Genesix come August? What did it reveal that, when she thought about it for one minute, she realized it would be far easier to lose touch with all of them after graduate school was done?

"Paleobiology," she said to Lionel, waving all of this away with the hand that wasn't holding her drink, "there isn't a future in it."

Lionel took off, excitedly, on a tangent, praising her choice to pursue biotech. He had a wholehearted earnestness that Naomi found admirable. Or she *wanted* to admire it. There were many promising offshoots blooming from the field, he was saying. The potential of resurrecting the clinically dead, of reanimating extinct species. And what luck for the world that she would be the captain of this marvelous ship, he concluded grandly.

She was tickled by his mixed metaphors, his overblown sense of her entry-level position. She understood that this man could love her, that he was eager to. And it could be easy to let him. Why not? She only had to give him an opening and he would take it. So she did laugh. At last. A true laugh. She laughed with him and at him, and she laughed at herself.

The music cut out abruptly and the woman was still laughing. It disarmed him, that laughter as it rang through the bar. He watched her and found nothing to say. She was even more beautiful when she was happy. He wanted to make her stay happy like this. Should he tell her that? Should he offer to buy her a drink? Should he ask for her number? He didn't usually feel this level of self-conscious anxiety in social situations. He began breathing heavily.

Lionel knew he would marry this woman. He knew it with a concrete and sudden certitude that dazzled him. He would marry her.

Only—what was her name?

It was biblical, he remembered. Old Testament. Mara? Or Leah? Ruth?

Naomi could not stop laughing. How much had she had to drink? Not much, it was not that. It was the blatant fact of Lionel's panic, adorable and plainly visible, and the absurdity of his being immediately enamored with her.

She thought, still laughing, that every detail of this night could become a story she might tell again and again: the story of how they first met. She could spend years with this man, a lifetime. She pictured her life married to this balding man, working in biotech, raising children. She imagined moving away from the bustle and crowds of Marks Island City, making a home in one of the quiet seaside suburbs. She would be happy. Because she could be if she chose to be.

She swallowed and heard the new song that was playing. It was by that handsome singer, Skip.

"Has anyone called you Skip before?" she said. "You look just like him." Lionel did not look very much like Skip. Perhaps slightly in the hairline and brow. But she said this regardless, hoping that, this way, they would remember the singer even if they both forgot which song of his was playing. "His wife is named Naomi too," she said, taking his hand.

Naomi! Lionel thought. Yes. Thank you, Naomi.

"Never," he said aloud.

He looked up at her. She looked down at his bald spot before she blinked it away.

If Evangeline and Maeve were, impossibly, to see their parents at this very moment, they'd recognize their father at once. The exact same expression he wore now would be frozen most of the time onto his face. But their mother, no. The twins would never believe their mother had been this person who, on a whim, blindly leapt over the boundary of being strangers toward the slim possibility of future happiness.

"Come on, Skip," Naomi said, pulling him gently. He placed the glass down. She would not call him Skip again. "Let's dance."

She imagined him with no mustache on their wedding day, standing at the end of the aisle, watching her. It made her giddy to see what might become a memory but hadn't yet happened. She liked it—she liked the way she pretended she'd feel.

IT WAS DIFFICULT TO keep track of which was which: Maeve and Evangeline. Evangeline and Maeve. The twins would hear their father's same jokes twice or not at all. If their mother was mad at one, she was mad at both. It wasn't just that they looked alike, though they were identical, but also that they occupied the same space in the same manner. They even sneezed in unison and, reopening their eyes, wore the exact same slightly surprised expression on their matching faces.

At age four, with their concept of self newly formed, the girls became fascinated with the bathroom mirror. Who was it inside there, her sister, herself, or a strange, silent triplet trapped in the glass?

By age five, they knew better. While they brushed their teeth at night, unblinking, the game was to pretend they were looking at their sister in the mirror until they felt a funny sensation in their body like they were neither here nor there but nowhere, everywhere.

At six, they had the same recurring night vision. It was not a full dream but a set of images that floated in and out in the moments before sleep arrived: the girl in the mirror spits her toothpaste into the sink while you are still brushing, she nods at you knowingly, waves, disappears.

Curious Critters was struggling. Admission fees were not enough to pay the rent on the museum. But Lionel's father gave him another loan and Naomi got a promotion, and they managed to keep it afloat.

Lionel took on extra work as an animal sideshow for birthday parties and spent weekends loading his dragonflies, beetles, and beloved ant terrarium into the station wagon. He set up a booth on a large, manicured backyard where, typically, his critters were one of several such attractions. There might be a face-painting station and other animals—ponies, parrots, a crocodile once, memorably. Whenever possible, he brought the twins along with him and they worked as his special assistants. The girls didn't care for this duty and found it weird to attend the birthdays of kids they'd never met.

Naomi worked long hours, commuting forty minutes from their suburban enclave of Jacob's Circle into the city, where she was the lead researcher. She hated the job and yet she buried herself in it and she had very little time to spend with her family.

They found a babysitter in the neighborhood and because of their work schedules, they came to rely on the girl fairly often. The babysitter had one of those faces that made it impossible to determine her age. She might have been sixteen or twenty-six.

Naomi took their daughters on the same outing every Saturday, when the weather allowed. Leaving Lionel at home to prepare for a birthday party or whatever it was he did in his office, she took the girls out to Rocky Beach for a dig.

The girls loved this tradition. They'd walk down the hill very early and stay until just before breakfast. They'd show their mother whatever they found, and she'd make the determination of what was worth keeping and what to toss back. She was especially looking for a certain kind of red rock. They'd found the right kind once and it had made their mother very happy. Digging was a mostly silent activity. There was the noise of seagulls and the rhythm of waves and it was calm and boring in a way the girls liked. "Therapeutic" was the word their mother used to describe it.

Once, they bumped into their mother's boss while digging. The girls knew very little about what their mother did. Just that she was very smart and very busy and a scientist.

"Dr. Wilhelm!" the man called from the boardwalk. He had been jogging with a puffy brown square of a dog. They could not see the dog's face for its puffiness. "Hello!" he said brightly. "Are these your children?"

The man was gigantic. He had shiny hair pushed back from his forehead by a neon-green sweatband. His arms were bulgy with muscles and his face was mean. He smiled at them and it made him look meaner.

"Yes," their mother said. "Maeve and Evangeline." She did not specify who was who.

"Twins!" said the man, thrilled. "Nature's clones!"

The girls glanced sideways at each other. Clones? What did that mean?

He stepped closer and they thought, horrified, that he was going to pet them, but a loud yipping began emanating from the dog, so the man bent to pet the animal instead.

The girls turned back to their digging and mostly stopped listening because the conversation made little sense.

"I see you've kept up your digging hobby," the man said near the end of the encounter. He was still smiling. He might have been making fun of their mother. They could not tell.

Their mother's lips thinned, and she angled her head at him.

"Enlisting child labor, though." He gestured toward the girls. "You know that's illegal, Naomi." He laughed.

Now, their mother put her shovel down, and for a second it seemed like she could burst out either screaming or laughing along with him.

"Oh, Dr. Dean," she said, "a lot of things are illegal."

They stared at each other without speaking, and soon after that, the man and his dog jogged away.

The girls did not ask their mother what being "a legal" was or "labor" or even "clones," which seemed most important. They kept digging a bit longer but no one found any red rocks. Their mother let them keep a smooth shard of blue sea glass and one stone in the exact shape of a heart. As the digging slowed, their mother stopped to look up and shield her eyes from the sun and stare, across the water, at Grace Beach over on Marks Island.

Eventually, the girls stopped digging also.

"Six today," they said as they packed up to leave. This was the final part of the Saturday ritual: the counting of fishing boats.

"Seven tomorrow," their mother would've replied. In the warmer months, every day brought more and more fishing boats to the harbor. In the cooler months, every day brought fewer and fewer.

Today, their mother must not have heard them, for she said nothing. Or she had heard them but simply forgotten the line she always said next.

IT HAD BEEN A snowy winter. The girls' mittens were too big and flapped over their fingertips uselessly. That was the bad part of this season. How your body got lost inside your clothes. Under their boots, the fresh snow made a noise like the garbage compactor.

"Hey," one sister said. "Watch this." She bent her knees deeply and jumped forward, springing up and out like a frog. When she landed, she was suspended. She stood on top of the whiteness before descending through the snow and touching back to earth.

"Try," her sister told her. She did.

So that was the day they hopped all over the front yard, feeling weightless and then weighted. It became the basis for two invented competitive winter games: long jump, in which they measured who could jump the farthest forward on the snow, and time jump, in which they measured how many seconds they could stay on top before it compacted and sent them down.

For time jump, Evangeline counted one one thousand, two one thousand while Maeve used Mississippis. And as far as measuring distance, they weren't very careful to have the same starting line. They weren't trying to win as much as they were trying to complete the challenge and look less like a dolt.

"Dolt" had been Maeve's contribution originally. Evangeline had gotten in trouble for saying the word "idiot," but Maeve had been allowed to say "dolt." So now it was "dolt" everything. "Oh dolt!" if they slipped and "Don't be a dolt."

They began racing, a good old-fashioned race from the tree to the mailbox. But a hopping race. The only way you could move was to keep your legs together and hop.

Occasionally, one of them would lose her balance, thrown off by the layers of clothing wrapped over her body.

When you fell, the rule was you had to get up with your legs together. It was extraordinarily difficult. Whenever one sister fell, the other stopped her racing to watch the struggle.

"You dolt!" she'd say. "Hurry! Get up! I'm going to win!"

Winning alone was not very fun, they'd found. There had to be at least some competition.

Inside the house, Naomi readied mugs of hot chocolate. The girls had been out there for an hour, which was too long. It did not matter how many layers of socks and sweatshirts they were wearing beneath their jackets and snow pants.

"Don't you think they should come in?" she said to Lionel. She could hear how taut her voice was. How close she was, already, to breaking. Why was she like this even on a cozy Sunday?

Lionel went to the window. He watched his daughters. What were they doing? Hopping as if in potato sacks, their hats falling over their eyes, lower and lower, both of their noses runny and red. Such strange little rabbits, his children.

"Give them another minute?" he said. It was his turn to be the parent to ruin their fun. He hated to do it.

"Fine."

They seemed to move in slow motion, with the labored movements of astronauts in low gravity. Each step, a small leap forward, then down.

Naomi still did not feel accustomed to it: her life as a wife, her life as a mother, her life generally. The twins were seven, which meant that for seven years, Naomi had daydreamed that somewhere, she had a twin too. A secret twin she hadn't known about who was living what should have been her own existence, one where everything that was misaligned for Naomi had fallen perfectly into place.

This secret, imaginary twin would be famous for her work on the ancient ecosystem of Marks Island. She'd have earned a place beside Dr. Francis Marks Sr. himself as one of the city's most notable residents. She'd be a tenured professor, the next chair of the department, blissfully childless, unmarried, alone. She'd have a lab at the city university named for her and a research hospital and a fellowship. What else?

Naomi had no twin, of course. Not even a sibling. And whenever she remembered this and floated back into her real life and saw it anew and as it was, she would think, incredulously, *This?* After everything, it all led to *this*?

There was Lionel with his bright mind but his dim wit and his expanding bald spot. Her girls, who were mostly afraid of her.

Her job. The fact that she was still at Genesix at all was unbelievable. Let alone that she'd moved up the corporate ladder to a senior title. It had happened with an ease she never suspected could bring success.

When she'd joined, there had been a thick veil of secrecy around her work and she couldn't see through it; her research team was not allowed to disclose anything, not even to the other research teams at their same arm of the company. She knew Genesix was racing two other biotech firms for a landmark discovery, but that was all she had known for close to a year.

She had been in Dr. Dean's office, sitting across from him. He always kept it dark in there and on that day, his eyes shined through the darkness and he wore that same smirk that made Naomi think of rigor mortis.

"A cure for age," he had said. "It's the next frontier for human ingenuity. There's no reason a body should have to suffer through time anymore. Picture it: a world where humans don't age."

He asked her to explain her graduate research and her model of ancient Marks Island.

"The algae," he said. "Tell me about *that*."

In truth, she was thrilled to talk about it again even though she had no idea what Dr. Dean was getting at or why he was interested. She explained the theory: that a unique species of alga once thrived in the water around Marks Island. Likely, it had been a keystone species, playing a crucial role in the ecosystem. It would have needed very large amounts of phosphorus to sustain a prolonged bloom. But she believed the island's coast had once been rich in that red mineral and—

"And is it still?" Dr. Dean asked, interrupting.

"We don't know for sure," she said. "There are traces that wash up every now and then, but we don't know how much of it might remain."

She explained that the same seismic activity that had shifted the landscape and attached the island to the mainland may have buried those deposits much deeper.

"I'm oversimplifying," she said, "and I should stress, again, that this was purely theoretical. More research was needed, more evidence." She paused. "I didn't really get to finish the project."

"So finish," he said.

"Excuse me?"

He'd already procured the approval from leadership, he told her. She could pick up where she had left off.

She was thrilled to hear this. Also confused.

"But what does my research have to do with an age cure?"

She'd crossed a line. She saw this at once. His eyes flashed and he made a tut-tut noise. "Oh, but you can't ask those kinds of questions, Dr. Wilhelm. That's the deal here. Okay?"

He could be so horribly patronizing. He might as well have been wagging a finger at her. But she wanted to return to her research. Okay, she told herself, she would be allowed to know some things, but not everything. She could live with that, couldn't she? She could live with a lot of things. That was something she'd learned.

"Yes," she said. "Sorry. Okay."

Her work would focus entirely on the ecosystem of ancient Marks Island. She would not do any of the digging, Dr. Dean explained. The land was restricted to a limited number of researchers. Another team would be collecting and testing the samples. That team would send her the relevant information and she would refine her computational model.

He had faith in her, he was saying. Full faith.

She thanked him for that because she could see she was supposed to.

“No need to thank me,” he said. “Just get to work.”

By all appearances, their competitors had outpaced them with other biotech breakthroughs—Xioneva had been testing an experimental cancer treatment for terminal patients and VextaGen announced their plan to transplant a human head—but Genesix remained single-minded, secretive, and set on the one mission: a cure for age.

Naomi was promoted to senior researcher but had no team working behind her. She was charged with her one small piece of an overall puzzle, a puzzle she still saw almost no details of, and she was not supposed to ask questions or share anything, not even with her own family.

Through the window, she watched her girls in the snow. Little aliens. She did not understand them, but they understood each other perfectly.

Lionel saw the lunar landscape they were making on the lawn. The girls were almost identical except for tiny discrepancies that had recently surfaced. He believed only he had observed them, for he'd been observing tiny discrepancies his entire professional life. One was proving to be ambidextrous and the other was not; one was slightly smaller than the other now, shorter and thinner at her knees and elbows especially.

He thought of mirror matter—that hypothetical substance that could explain away the asymmetry of the universe. He could still get lost in the riddles of astrophysics. Like parallel universes, and the Fermi paradox, or the twin paradox, which was one of his favorites.

In another moment, he would get up and put on his coat and go out there to get them. He might play with them after they taught him the rules for this game they'd invented. But just briefly. After that, he would have to give them the bad news. The day was ending, and it was time to come in. They would protest and get one more game out of him. "One game, that's it," he would say. But it would not be it.

Eventually, Naomi would have to go outside herself, jacket unzipped, standing on the snowy steps in her slippers, and call for him.

"Lionel!" she'd yell. "What are you doing?" But she wouldn't be angry. She'd just want an invitation.

So he would invite her. He could see it all playing out: Lionel would get Naomi to play the game too. She'd disappear for a second and reappear with her boots and they'd hop around the lawn together, racing, falling over, calling each other dolts, until the sky was dark and the day really ended and, cold and exhausted, they went inside.

The mugs of hot chocolate would be cold and in need of reheating. Everyone's sopping socks would be hung out to dry. Each of them would remember this.

Everything was in the process of ruin, Naomi thought as she watched her girls' booted feet make divots in what might have remained an unblemished stratum of white for at least the one evening.

She imagined her former excavation site on Grace Beach and how it might have looked now according to the rumors of what Genesix was doing. Usually, corporate leadership did a good job of tamping such rumors down. But this gossip was pervasive. Naomi couldn't say where she had first heard it. Once you learned a thing like that, it rooted down as a fact.

Genesix had made a deal with the Marks Foundation to dispose of their biowaste off the shores of Marks Island. There was no environmental impact committee involved, no telling how the ancient land would be ruined. That was what the rumor held.

Was that why she'd been asked to continue refining her models of the ancient ecosystem? To predict just what they were destroying? And was that why she had not been permitted to collect the samples herself? They didn't want her to see what else was out there. The idea that she might have been part of this—helping to ruin the very land that had been the focus of all her academic research—once it occurred to her, she became obsessed with it. She had to know.

The rumor kept simmering through the fall and now winter, and still, no one on the executive team addressed it. Genesix had a punitive policy on the books to prevent employees from speaking ill of the company. It had been enforced in the past and Naomi kept waiting to hear of someone being suspended or fired or held accountable for starting this gossip, and yet no one was.

Naomi assumed this was because Genesix was finally close to their breakthrough. They didn't have to bother with petty rumors. The company had sent out a short brief about it; they would soon seek approval to bring their antiaging procedure to market.

Dr. Dean had been promoted to chief marketing officer, an advancement that Naomi fully expected would be a brief stop on his hoped-for journey to become chief executive of the company.

The "age cure," she learned in the brief, would be an injectable. It would stop the physical process of aging, keeping a person looking the same age indefinitely.

As a secondary use, it was found to be moderately successful at reducing pain. People would need to have the injection monthly. Naomi guessed Genesix could have made it a one-time procedure, had they calibrated it slightly differently, but that was not good for business. To get around some legal requirements, they would brand the procedure as cosmetic. It was almost laughable to remember, but she had thought they were coming up with a *cure* for something.

The girls must be freezing. What was Lionel doing? He was supposed to call them in a half hour ago.

"Time to come in," Lionel said to them again when, after thirty minutes, Naomi still had not joined them.

A breath of silence.

His daughters looked at him, at each other, at him again, preparing to argue or at least considering it. They wanted to keep playing. But who knew what kind of mood their mother was in.

Back inside, they took off their wet boots and socks and changed into warm pajamas. They meant to write down the rules of their made-up games but they forgot to, and then it was bedtime, and soon they forgot the rules and the games entirely. It did not snow again for the rest of the winter, so it didn't matter in the end.

THE TRAFFIC INTO THE city was worse in the springtime. There were more tourists, plus the snowbirds who'd escaped for the season returned. Naomi's morning commute could take twice as long, and she'd get to the office edgy to a point very close to combustion and desperate for a cigarette. She had mostly quit. She only smoked at work.

"It'd be faster to swim," her secretary would say whenever he could read on her face that the traffic had been unbearable. He'd hand her a coffee, and she'd grunt at him.

It was, in a way, a class distinction. Only those with senior roles could complain of the traffic, for they were the ones who lived outside the city. They each had their oversized home and big backyard, with swing sets and a neighborhood golf course or clubhouse or pool. The rest of the employees—the entry-level staff and lower-level managers and certainly all the secretaries—lived a crowded, urban existence, crammed into tiny apartments with too many roommates like Lionel's little boxes of bugs.

On a bright June morning, a particularly bad accident in the tunnel made the seven-mile drive take nearly two hours.

"It'd be faster to swim."

When he said it that time, she heard him. She had a momentary urge to pour the scalding cup in his face. What was wrong with him? She did not need his sympathy over something as trivial and meaningless as traffic in the tunnel. What was wrong with *her*?

Sitting down at her desk, she really thought about it. Swimming. It was probably three miles from Rocky Beach to Grace Beach. That was all. It would have been another mile, walking, soaking wet, along the coast of the former island across the isthmus, to the Genesix office downtown on the mainland.

But she wasn't thinking of swimming to work; she was thinking of swimming to Grace Beach.

The procedure had a name now: Prosyntus, whatever that meant. It would be released early, thanks to someone at Food and Drug who owed them a favor. All the executives got a big bonus and Genesix's stock soared, and now they could all just relax and celebrate. That was the idea. She would be put on a new project soon.

After the final approval, she'd asked Dr. Dean about the rumors directly. He wasn't her boss anymore. Why did she still find him so threatening?

"Is it true," she asked, "about the waste site? On Marks Island?"

He didn't look an hour older than he had when she'd first met him. She wondered if Dr. Dean had found the cure for aging long ago and kept it to himself. But his lips pulled back and his teeth showed, and there it was, written all over the outside edges of his features: time.

"Now, Doctor," he said, not missing a beat, "why would we do something like that?"

She had the strange idea that he was genuinely happy to hear that this rumor was still alive and in circulation.

She had not been on Grace Beach since the morning of the awards ceremony back in graduate school. She'd just earned her PhD and had her paper published and she'd feared intensely that her dream was ending.

She came out that day for one last dig, and she stood near the rim of the excavation site. She'd said a kind of prayer of mourning for what she had found and what she would never find inside it, and she'd gone for a swim.

Naomi remembered this as she woke before sunrise to swim out there. She remembered these things, but she couldn't really remember being the person who had done them. It was more like a memory of watching a twin.

Really, it was hard to believe she'd wanted the things she had wanted so ravenously and for so long, and all for what?

She slipped into the one wet suit she had kept from her swimming days. It was snug but not terrible. She found the waterproof pack that buckled around her waist. Lionel snored on, unbothered. She felt ridiculous. Like a whale with a fanny pack.

Her plan was simple. She would swim out to Grace Beach and find the waste site. She might collect samples for testing, then swim home.

She prepared herself for what she thought she would find out there: industrial pipes pouring sludge into the water, a shoreline coated in grime, a minefield of dead sea stars with their insides leaking out and limbs missing, the choking smell of rot. She closed her eyes. The noise of the machinery. She supposed she'd hear the noise of it all first.

What would she do after bringing the samples back to the lab and testing them for toxins? She wasn't sure. All she wanted was to know what role she'd played in all of it.

Naomi did not believe in god. She considered herself too much of a scientist and a cynic all her life to practice religion. But Marks Island was an ancient place, and this made it sacred to her. Thousands of years ago, humans had called that land home. A tribe of diggers, like her.

A few hundred feet from Grace Beach, there were caves that this tribe had dug. No one knew why or what the caves were for, though there were theories. The Marks Foundation had, in the years since she'd last been out there, built an entire museum around the caves.

Dr. Francis Marks Sr. had named the caves for his wife: the Caves of Adina. But Adina Marks was a mostly hidden figure in the many biographies of Dr. Marks. If she appeared at all, she was painted in an archetypal light: a silent, suffering wife who'd been widowed young.

Naomi had read these biographies in graduate school. She'd been drawn to the near absence of Adina Marks. There was one quote in one chapter of one book that had stayed with Naomi because it showed a glimpse of a different woman altogether.

Asked what she thought of the caves being named for her, Adina Marks had answered, "There is no knowing what the ancient people first called the caves. There's no knowing what they called anything. Sometimes, I think we should stop giving new names to very old things. Sometimes, I wonder if the most accurate history is the one that remains unclaimed and untold."

This was what Naomi's prayer consisted of that last time she had been out there: trying to rid herself of all the new names that had been used to classify very old things. Trying to rid herself of the urge to know and claim. Praying that she could let go. Stop seeking. Choose, for once, to just be.

And maybe that was what Dr. Dean had meant?

You can be happy if you decide to be.

She said this to herself over and over as she swam, the rhythm of her breathing carrying her across the water. It was a longer, harder swim than she had anticipated. She arrived on Marks Island exhausted and rolled out on the beach and looked up at the sky.

In a moment, when she caught her breath again, she'd find the waste site. She'd collect as many samples as she thought she could carry for the swim home. She would hate to see how this sacred land was being ruined by science. And so she didn't get up to see it, not yet.

She looked at the sky and not at the sand or any of the solid bits of rock that formed this mass of land that had once been an island in one of the planet's vast oceans.

She stayed still another moment, not knowing how much destruction she'd helped bring in, unwittingly or, really, in the selfish pursuit of her own narrow scholarly interest, her own oversized ambition. She let the water lap up under her.

Slowly, a sound broke through her reverie. Not a sound but a silence. She heard the waves and the wind and some insects, but there was no noise of machinery. She smelled no rot as she breathed. Maybe Genesix wasn't dumping anything? Maybe it was all just a rumor after all?

She sat up and the sea sparkled before her.

In the distance, she saw something. What was it? Just beyond the back of the museum. There it is, she thought. And her heart beat madly. But what was it? It didn't appear equipped to dump waste into the ocean. It looked more like it might be *extracting* something. Yes, it looked, Naomi thought, like a mining rig.

What was Genesix doing?

Questions were dawning on her that she already knew the answers to. Had they let the rumor flourish because it helped them to hide the truth? Had they even started the rumor themselves? Had they been the ones to spread it?

Naomi hadn't noticed the algae as she swam. It had been floating in a patch far from where she'd surfaced for air. Even now, as she gazed out, the twinkling on the sea looked to be just the sunlight reflecting. But when she waded out toward the vessel, she saw it all around her: it was thick, red, and phosphorescent.

THE NEIGHBORS CHATTED IN low voices near mailboxes, over hedges, and between pickets of fences; at the ends of driveways while taking the garbage out; and on sidewalks as they untangled the leashes of dogs who wanted to play.

The information circulated all around Jacob's Circle, the soft whisper of the word "suicide" swirling with the warm June breeze.

Dr. Wilhelm—the mother—was dead.

It turned out that somebody knew somebody who had known her in college—not a close friend, but they'd known her enough to know that she could swim. That she had been a swimmer, and not just in a leg of the relay either; she'd been an open-water, long-distance swimmer. And this detail made her apparent suicide by drowning much stranger.

Though perhaps, they theorized, anyone was capable of drowning herself if she tried hard enough?

That night, lying awake, these neighbors turned the details over. Dr. Wilhelm had been found with rocks in her pockets, the newspaper said.

The next day was the first Saturday of summer, and the beach club for Jacob's Circle residents was open for the season. The sun was high and hot and the neighbors sat on beach chairs, sweating.

They pooled what they knew. It was very little, troublingly little. It seemed no one had talked to Dr. Wilhelm about anything beyond the smallest of neighborly talk. They tried to trace back at least the one fact they'd gleaned—whose cousin's friend or friend's cousin was it who'd attended college with the late doctor? The path kept ending in circles.

In all fairness, they told each other, Dr. Wilhelm had not been an easy person to get to know. She was reserved. "Aloof," was the word they'd thought privately. This, they'd always figured, was her problem—hers, and not theirs. Now, they thought maybe this was the problem all along. The Reason. Or one of the reasons, at least. Since, surely, there was more than one reason a person chose to end her life? Who could say? They could not, yet they kept trying to.

"Apparent suicide," the newspaper had called it. What did they mean by that, they wondered, "apparent"?

Every so often someone would turn to glance over a shoulder and check that the Wilhelms, the father and daughters, were not approaching.

The Wilhelm family never came to the beach club, the others reminded.

And even if they did, would they have expected the family to come to a beach club on this, the very morning after the mother's apparent suicide?

They agreed, she had been intimidating: smart, serious, beautiful with those curls and her cool expression. They knew she worked around the clock. And though she'd never joined them here at the beach club—not at the snack bar with its limited offerings, not at either of the two pools, the big kids' or the kiddie pool, as the children called them, and not at the clean, secluded strip of shoreline accessible only to them, these lucky residents of Jacob's Circle—she did take her girls on Saturday mornings down the hill to Rocky Beach. That public strip off the main road beside the harbor. The neighbors had seen the pack of three returning before 9:00 a.m., dry but carrying pails and towels, flip-flops trailing sand in their wake.

Why would anyone choose Rocky Beach when she could have come here, with them, to a private beach club? This was another mystery they would never get to the bottom of.

Rocky Beach was where it had happened though. A fisherman had found her.

The Wilhelm father, he was quite the oddball.

They discussed it again the next morning, a Sunday, back at the club.

Even in grief, they had seen, as he waved hello from his car, passing the security gate, he had the same goofy expression. And he'd always had that general overeagerness that made them, in retrospect, marvel at the mismatch between husband and late wife.

The children were twins. Identical. It was impossible to tell them apart and so they did not bother trying.

Throughout the start of summer, these whispers about the family continued at the beach club. But there was little more to say. From the outside, by all appearances, they were still a functioning household. Nothing a neighbor might think to complain about. No loud arguments. No overgrown lawns. No long-term guests who parked awkwardly, unused to the rounded curb of the circle. Nor did the neighbors learn much more about the mother or what The Reason or The Reasons might have been.

Eventually, the neighbors concluded that these things just happen.

Other gossip emerged. The weather turned cool. It became autumn. The beach club closed and would remain closed until the next season.

And so again, the newest news was circulated over mailboxes and hedges and between the pickets of fences, at the ends of driveways as they took the garbage out, and on sidewalks as the leashes of their dogs kept tangling, no matter how firmly they commanded the playful pets to heel.

-3-

A QUARTER CENTURY OF SLEEP

NO MAJOR EARTHQUAKE HAS BEEN ACCURATELY PREdicted. The best one can do is predict the statistical likelihood at a certain location over a certain time.

At this specific location and at this specific time, the likelihood is increasing as a man with perfect posture stands in front of the caves. He gives his welcome, which consists of simple statements of logic.

"She remembers how to breathe. Therefore, she remembers."

This resonates with the former Congregants. After all, they are forgetters and they are forgotten.

"She remembers how to sleep. Therefore, she remembers."

It resonates with the others too. Everyone holds on to memories that they desperately don't want forgotten while, at the same time, desperately needing *not* to be the ones who must go on remembering them.

"And she does not age," he says. "Therefore, she will go on this way: sleeping, breathing, and remembering."

Each member of the audience was invited to bring along an object. He explains that as part of the ceremony, they will each have their turn to stand in the caves with the sleeping child. They will place their offerings next to her, and this is how, together, they will create their Archive of Sleep.

The offerings are also petitions. They are asking the sleeping child to remember these nearly lost artifacts of their nearly lost lives.

As he speaks, the crowd finds their objects in their pockets and purses. They do not need them yet. But they enjoy holding them this final time before they will part with them. They rub them gently between their fingers and they pass them from hand to hand.

–4–

One year into Maeve's sleep

ON THEIR TRIP TO THE CANYON, TESS STARTED CALLing herself "Dying Tess" again, as if terminal illness transformed her into a new person entirely.

She told Luke, "You don't like Dying Tess," as she put her coat on. It wasn't a question.

"I love Dying Tess," he clarified, and he kissed her.

But as they found their car in the motel parking lot, he thought more about it. He decided they were both right.

At Luke's worst, Tess's decision to die felt like a choice to also very slowly break up with him and never see him again. They were each in pain, said this worst part of him, but she was luckier because her pain would end.

At his best, he could see how horrible a thought that was. He disliked Dying Tess, but he hated the version of himself that was with Dying Tess much, much more.

And who was that?

That was just Plain Old Luke.

Anyway, Dying Tess was the same Tess she'd always been, he thought, and he meant that in the best way. Even now—more than three years into her sickness—she was the Tess he'd first met:

teasingly wonderful or else righteously indignant. It was only the dynamic between the two of them that had changed very much. And not since her diagnosis either, but since Tess wrote The List.

Now, it was like they were standing on the cliff edge of a terrible emptiness together. An abyss was before them, and they kept leaning toward it and not falling in.

She had to feel it too, he assumed, the urge to jump already.

As they merged onto the highway, Tess said, "I think I need to throw up," and she rolled down her window.

They'd been driving for three days, stopping at motels along the route. Tess had puked twice but managed, so far, not to puke in the car. Luke got off at an exit.

"False alarm," she said the next moment.

They passed a sign for a diner. "Let's stop there for lunch?" She rolled the window back up. "I'm famished."

"Okay," he breathed. He did not look at her. He felt dizzied by the swings in her status, from almost puking to ravenous.

"I know," she said, smiling. "It's a weird back-and-forth."

Luke and Tess were both drawn to old things. At home, their furniture was mostly antique, and their bookshelves were lined with historical tomes. They found it funny when retro became trendy again. The new spins people put on the same old classics, making them not the same old classics at all.

The restaurant was one of those retro diners that had been popular for a while. Luke had eaten with Tess at dozens of similar spots. Tess had a list of them in her notebook because they used to try out a new one basically every Sunday. They'd go in for lunch and start looking for where, exactly, it had failed at any attempt at accurate historical re-creation.

Usually, it was the menu first and foremost. There might be one small section for "classic fare"—egg creams, root beer floats—and the rest was taken up by artisan salads with a dozen ingredients in the dressing alone.

But this particular diner right off the highway seemed like it could be authentic. Luke wouldn't have been able to say why, and he knew he might be imagining it, but he couldn't help wondering if the place might have survived long enough to come back in style. Did that happen? There was the soda fountain. The Formica. The peeling red vinyl of the booth where they were seated.

For a minute, he could see the scene as it might have been once, long ago: waitresses roller-skating with trays of milkshakes, their ponytails swaying while a jukebox played rock and roll in a corner, Tess in a blouse with a Peter Pan collar. A poodle skirt. Did anyone ever really wear poodle skirts?

He let himself pretend that they were living there, in that era, real or imagined. Or in a more recent past; back in their old lives at home in their apartment in Marks Island City, before they knew the source of Tess's headaches, or—better yet—before those headaches had begun.

He saw Tess look up at the restaurant for the first time and take it all in. She must be thinking it too, he guessed.

She pulled out her notebook and added this one to that long list of diners, and she stared at Luke as though daring him.

She said, "This one is a particularly bad replica, right?"

WHEN TESS FIRST BECAME sick, there were all these scientific advancements being announced to great fanfare. Three biotech companies had opened branches in the city, and their names were futuristic and easily interchangeable: Genesix, Xioneva, VextaGen.

"Signs of the end times," Tess would say whenever technology was getting ahead of itself.

She kept a list of ominous headlines. It started with "Extinct Animal Cloned."

Biotech researchers had reanimated fossilized DNA from a woolly mammoth. The cloned animal was born in one of the shiny new research facilities downtown, not far from their apartment.

On his way to work in the mornings, Luke would bike by the line of reporters, all waiting in the lot of the office park so they might catch one of the scientists and try to get a comment.

Their news cameras were lightweight and sleek. They made the medium-format that Luke carried in its own pack with all its separate attachments feel like an artifact, which in some ways it was. Nobody used that kind of camera anymore.

The woolly mammoth was named Dolly Jr. after the famous cloned sheep, and she was held in a pen where visitors could see her. The big debate wasn't over Dolly herself but whether to bring back a male and revive the species.

They went to see her once. They felt sorry for Dolly and they wanted to apologize on behalf of all people. This was before Tess's surgery but after the surgery date had been scheduled. A strange period when all they could do was wait and pretend their lives weren't just hanging in the balance.

"Nobody asks to be born," Tess said, staring at the enormous mammal, "or to be born again."

"There's such loneliness in being the last of your kind," Luke said.

Already, they were talking past each other.

They watched the animal for about a half hour. Her eyes were big black marbles. Wet and melancholy. As if she might start to weep at any moment, releasing tears so big they would splash back up from the ground.

"The lonely mammoth," Tess said. Then, turning to Luke, "There's a good title."

Visitors weren't supposed to take pictures but nobody stopped him or said anything when he snapped one of Dolly with Tess in half-light at her side.

"The Lonely Mammoth," she wrote down in her notebook under a list she kept of good titles for his photographs.

Aside from their love of antiques, Luke and Tess were opposites in most ways.

He worked in advertising, and she worked for a human rights organization. That meant Tess helped create new lives for refugees, and Luke helped create maybe the one thing that could always leave people a little less fulfilled: longing.

They used to joke about it. A marriage of late-stage capitalism, they said. They couldn't afford to both work to make the world a better place, right? One of them had to pay the bills and make the world slightly worse. It might balance out, their karma.

There were other things too. Like, Luke talked about his job all the time and Tess hardly spoke of hers, preferring—he assumed—to save him the heartache. He could always tell when her job was taxing her, but he almost never knew why. She spent large swaths of her day interviewing asylum seekers, hearing their horrors.

She had been obsessed for a few years with a very small island. Palmavja, it was called, and though it was not far away, Luke might not have been able to find it on a map before Tess pointed it out to him.

Tess had helped a refugee woman from Palmavja to resettle. The woman was young and had lost everything, her whole family. "She is trying to make a life as an artist now," Tess told him.

It made Tess furious how the news wouldn't cover the violence there and how little anyone seemed to care about the history of the island or what was happening on the island right now.

"What *is* happening now?" Luke asked. He genuinely wanted her to tell him so that he could feel angry over something—anything—more meaningful than a fast-food chain using a slogan too similar to the one he'd just pitched for a high-end clothing brand's fall campaign.

There was an aquatic plant with a name that translated to "briar palm," she explained. It was ancient and it had grown only off Palmavja's shores.

A generation ago, a potent painkiller had been derived from it. The drug was illegal and intravenous and highly addictive, injected with a syringe in the crook of an elbow until that region was decimated. After that, one could try the underside of a tongue, the thin skin between toes.

"You'd try to pierce a vein," Tess said, "anywhere a vein still surfaced."

The side effects included memory loss, coma, aggressive infection at the injection site that could spread to the spine. Overdose. In time, to use it more brought you less pleasure and to use it less brought you more pain.

"I bet," she said, pausing in her recounting, "you would like to ask me what the government did to stop it, right?"

Luke could hear the irony in Tess's voice. He nodded anyway.

Palmavja was, at that time, ruled by a dictator, she explained. And he came to power not in spite of his ties to the drug cartels but because of them. So he ignored and dismissed the scope of this epidemic right up until the day his only son died from it.

"And then he sprang into action."

He criminalized addiction, placing sufferers in for-profit prisons. He made a show of cracking down on the cartels by arresting a single, albeit notorious, drug lord. But mostly, Tess told him, sounding exhausted, he targeted the native community, who suffered most from the crisis. He sent in armed troops and limited their freedoms of mobility and privacy and bodily autonomy.

People took to the streets to protest, and state-run media labeled these "riots." Tensions escalated, and the dictator sanctioned the use of his most destructive weapons against his own people.

The epidemic did end, but only because briar palm was said to be depleted. After that, the dictator was overthrown and democracy came, and everyone tried to restore and forget.

"And now?" Luke asked.

"And now, as you might guess, briar palm's back."

The way Tess told him all this, it seemed like an old and predictable story. Another epidemic raged, the drug having returned in a new form as a perfectly legal prescription pill.

"And so on and so on," she said.

She showed him a photograph the woman at the refugee center had given her. She said it had been passed around on Palmavja—that the democratic government had tried hard to censor it. But she'd escaped with dozens of copies.

It was a wide-angle landscape with rows and rows of unfilled graves. Corpses with bluish complexions lay inside them, facing up.

For a second, Luke couldn't help but envy the photographer for the composition. But he remembered not to envy anyone who was there to document this tragedy.

"Why aren't the graves filled?" he asked softly.

"Cemeteries are public land," Tess told him, "but there aren't enough gravediggers left to do the work of filling them fast enough. Also the soil froze early. The island gets a lot of seismic activity and there's an old superstition that moving the earth can trigger a quake. So when the soil is frozen, they won't try to move it until it thaws again. Usually, there aren't so many graves left open, and usually they don't look . . . like that."

Most of the corpses had their eyes open. Luke stared at them.

An icy hand formed a fist inside his stomach. This was what Tess walked around with all the time. He felt closer to her momentarily.

AT THE DINER NEAR the canyon, Luke ordered a cup of orzo soup that was goopy and tepid, and Tess got three hot dogs loaded up with the usuals—ketchup, mustard, relish—and some strange stuff, too—liquid cheese, potato sticks, bits of bacon, small and pink and burnt like eraser dust.

He watched her take turns taking bites of each until Tess said, "Take a photo. You can call it *Dying Tess, with Hot Dogs.*"

He laughed a hollow laugh and Tess paused chewing to pose. When he took the picture, the camera whirled and whirled and he thought: Damn. Automatic rewind.

"That was the last photo of the last roll of film," he said. He felt choked up about this, strangely.

The manufacturer had stopped making film for this camera years ago. So that was the last of this camera also. It was always going to happen. He held it in his hands and banged it against the table edge once and not hard.

In his mind, he took a quick inventory of every photo he'd taken on their road trip. A part of him would spend the rest of their visit to the canyon finding the moments he most resented having no way to frame and to freeze.

"WHY DON'T YOU TRY *living* your life?" Tess had said to him, teasing.

When this last stretch of her illness began and they knew it was only a matter of time, all he had been able to do was take photos. She was right. It wasn't like that camera—or anything else—could change the future that was rapidly approaching.

But her question stung, and he came up with a mean response he almost spat back. He bit his tongue and turned away from her.

Tess said it for him anyway, making it into one of her jokes.

She said, "Try living? I know what you must be thinking. 'Speak for yourself.'"

When Tess learned she was dying, she chose to die.

This had become a refrain Luke repeated to keep from pointing his anger at her directly. It made it clear that it wasn't much of a choice at all. Not an "if." Just a "when."

The surgery didn't cure her, and the radiation didn't cure her, and the tumors kept growing. Her long hair fell out, and even her fingers looked skinny. There was one experimental treatment she might have still had—she was a perfect candidate—but she turned it down because, in the best case, it might extend her life another small fraction. Her cancer was going to kill her. Nobody denied that.

If it were him, Luke knew, he would have kept fighting for another second until no more seconds were left. He didn't think this would be brave. It was just what he would do. He'd probably knock on the doors of all three biotech facilities, desperate, begging for anything they could offer him no matter the cost.

But it wasn't him. It was Tess. And so here they were, completing The List by seeing the canyon.

"I only have so much time," she'd said to him. "I don't want to waste it by pretending that isn't true."

Tess promised that she wouldn't take the medicine that would kill her immediately after they saw the canyon. Even though the canyon was the last item on The List. She said she'd wait a little bit longer. She'd assured him of that. She hadn't even brought the pills on the trip with them. Otherwise, Luke would never have wanted to go.

But she still could not decide when exactly she would die, and this was frustrating to him. Not knowing, even now, just how close they were to the end. Or how far away.

No one knew, Tess would point out if he complained to her.

That was true. Still, he resented that she knew some things and not everything.

They had shared many moments of light even in sickness. There had always been moments of light with Tess. It was just who she was, dying or not.

Like the time, right before her surgery, when she saw that older surgeon with no sense of humor.

She said to him, "Something's wrong with my head, Doc."

The doctor said, very serious and condescending to make sure that Tess understood him, "Yes, dear. We know, we'll try hard to fix that."

She shook it, stubbornly. "Don't bother. This one's giving me all kinds of trouble. Let's just try one a half size up."

The wrinkled skin above the doctor's nose ironed out and miraculously, the man smiled.

"That might have been his first smile," Luke said later, "in decades."

"Oh, easily," Tess replied. "I have that effect on people."

At different points in the last three years, they'd even had hope too. He could remember the feeling of that.

There was a long stretch of it before they came to the canyon; she didn't get better but nothing worsened, and this bought them so much more time than they'd ever thought they'd have. And earlier, too, near the very beginning, they were allowed to believe that the single surgery could be the whole of the story.

"This will be the worst part," they told themselves and each other. "After this, it gets better."

When she'd checked into the hospital, they gave her a crazy consent form. It was two inches thick with tiny type, no page numbers, too much legal language to try to decipher. But that was fine because they did not try to decipher it. It was, to them both, a beautiful piece of bureaucracy that held the key to her health. Like some age-old, sacred healing ritual.

He took a picture of her in her gown on the hospital bed as she signed it.

She kept calling the consent form "the release" and saying dramatically, "It will release me, Luke."

Release you from what? he wondered. To where?

NOT LONG AFTER THE birth of the cloned woolly mammoth, there was a second local scientific breakthrough when a human head was successfully transplanted. Luke thought this was a grotesque advancement: a healthy head and brain from one dying body grafted onto another person's spinal cord. Nonetheless, you could have a second life now in a new body. That was, if you were lucky and it wasn't your brain that was killing you.

He thought of Tess's joke to the surgeon as he read all about the new technology, and Tess added the article to her list of ominous news.

A part of him could see the appeal of it though. If you didn't think too hard about this stuff, and most people did not, there was a would-be-nice idea of immortality floating around. The city was bustling with the new industry of biotech, and Luke's client list shifted. Every day brought a new initiative to convince the public that death no longer had to have its constant stranglehold over life.

Sometimes, when he was working late on a project, it seemed impossible that a tiny mass of cells could destroy someone. After all, We Live in the Future Now, as all the ad copy he was drafting would claim. Other times, he felt the pulse of his and Tess's outsider status. He could picture himself with his artifact of a camera and Tess with her archaic illness and it seemed obvious that the future had gone on without them; that they belonged, instead, to a more terrifying and primitive time.

There were rumors of another medical advancement; a procedure that would stop the body from aging. Luke came to the office one day and this was the only thing his coworkers wanted to talk about. They speculated about how much it would cost and when they would know if Genesix, the company developing it, would sign on with them.

Luke was quiet, listening.

He was known in the office as a bit of a Luddite. He loved discussing his collection of antique cameras, which included the medium-format but also camcorders and cameras with handheld flashes and folding accordion cameras and one kinetoscope, even.

But he could also recognize the fine line between old-fashioned and outdated, and he knew, professionally, how to stand squarely on the right side of that line and use it to his advantage.

He had won over clients with what his manager called his "authentically retro sensibility." He could speak passionately about the difference between filters designed to look old and photographs that were, in actuality, old. And he could wait patiently until others saw that distinction and accept when they decided they'd go with the newer tech anyway because the difference was so slight and it was so much less expensive that way.

When Genesix did sign on with his firm, they asked Luke to lead their campaign.

In the first conversation he had with them, the chief marketing officer stressed the need to tie the procedure back to something comfortable, known.

"Make it seem less scary," the CMO said.

"Roger that, boss," Luke replied, and he gave a thumbs-up.

"How's that Fountain of Youth doohickey?" his colleagues asked a few weeks into the project. They often did these exaggerated impressions of Luke's old-timey slang.

He played along. "Why, it's the bee's knees," he told them.

But the procedure was still nameless. What was he supposed to do with that? He'd asked for an update four times already, and he had a weird feeling that they might have already chosen a name and direction without him and did not want to tell him. Or else, something bad was going on and advertising was the least of Genesix's concerns. No one had called him back and he had only the one point of contact. The CMO, a broad man with swollen-seeming hands.

"The cat's pajamas," a coworker said, slapping him on the shoulder a little too hard.

That same night when he got home Tess told him what she'd learned a whole three weeks earlier. The tumors had spread. He'd been so busy with work, she said. She had struggled to find the right time to tell him.

There was more, too: she was choosing to die.

There was the experimental option, she explained, but it wouldn't be a cure—only a delay. And it might not work at all. It was more likely to leave her suffering delusions.

"I can deal with the pain," she said.

Plus, she'd rather not keep postponing the inevitable. She'd rather just enjoy what they had left.

"Clear-eyed" was the phrase she kept using.

The first thought Luke had was of the CMO. He remembered the man's one instruction: "Make it seem less scary." It was all he could think of to say, so he said nothing. They stared at each other for several long seconds before he looked away.

IN THE LAST PHOTO of his last roll of film there would be mustard stained on Tess's chin forever, and Luke would be stunned by it—how she still looked beautiful to him while dying in a diner. He'd never be able to bear saying a single word about that out loud.

Tess took a final bite of a hot dog, and she burped, loud. She wiped her face with a napkin, erasing the mustard blot. Her eyes focused on the blank space above him.

"It's such a joy," she said as though accepting an award, "to get to eat hot dogs without worrying about the junk inside them." Her laughter shook her thin body and a crumb of bacon fell from her lip onto her plate.

WHY DON'T YOU TRY living your life? It had been a rhetorical question. But he could have answered it.

Because I'm too busy trying not to break down crying all the time.

Because it is actually *our* life, Tess, that you're ending.

Because when I look at you, sitting across from me, eating hot dogs, laughing at your own special brand of gallows humor, I see a sepia tone bleed into your face, bathing you, already, in a pool of nostalgia and time.

IT WAS ONLY A few miles to the canyon and Tess drove. In the passenger seat, Luke took out The List. Soon, he'd cross out the very last item and this list would be done.

"What do you think?" she said, looking over at him. "Time for another?"

It was the kind of joke that he hated because if he were being honest, yes. Start a new list. It didn't have to be over. Not yet.

"Yes, please," he said, and he watched her droop a little.

For as long as he'd known Tess, she had kept lists for everything.

She had a list of movies with snakes in them and a list of movies in which a man said to a woman, "Don't worry, I've got this." She had a list of restaurants with incomprehensible descriptions of food on the menu and a list of restaurants where menu items were numbered so you could just say to a waiter, "I'll take the number eight." She had a list of books with strangely wide margins and a list of novels with very short chapters.

This was another way in which they were opposites. When packing for a trip, Luke preferred to spread all possible items out in an array so that he could see them together, hold every item against every other, and in that way decide which things he needed most to bring: this pair of warm socks or this extra sweater; this thick book he was almost done reading or this thin paperback he had yet to start and might hate.

Tess, on the other hand, had her list to work from. She hunted through the apartment holding the page in her hand, tracking down the items in the order they first came to her mind and were documented: bug spray in the downstairs bathroom, cargo shorts in the bedroom, travel pillow in the hall closet.

Each of them made the other crazy this way. Tess cringed at the mess he made just to pack for a weekend. Luke felt anxious from her hurried pacing upstairs and downstairs, back and forth.

When she made her decision and stopped trying new treatments, Tess wrote a list of things that made her feel good. This led to the list of things that might make her feel good, and that was the list that became The List, capital *L*, the list of things she still wanted to do with Luke.

As they waited in a line of cars to pay their admission, Luke pictured the very near future. He'd have The List, and he'd have dozens of canisters of film to develop in the darkroom, and he'd have souvenirs and brochures and ticket stubs that they'd collected along the way. He could spread this all out to form a last array on their bedroom floor. He might stand on the desk and take a photograph looking down to capture all of it. He might hold every item in that pile up and remember it. He would wish he could bring them all with him wherever he went from then on.

It would be, he felt, a very long trip he'd have to go on without her.

THE FIRST ITEMS ON The List were close, so they had stayed in and around town for a long while. They'd visited local tourist attractions, monuments and museums that they could have seen any old day and so they'd never seen once.

They went to the Marks Museum of Human History and spent one Sunday morning learning about a far more distant past than the one they typically found themselves drawn to: the ancient humans who'd made that land home.

Tess and Luke went inside the Caves of Adina, where the prehistoric humans were found. Afterward Tess spoke to the museum owner. He was the grandson of the famous scientist who'd found the tribe, and they spoke for a long while about the possibilities of what those caves may have been for. Luke found the man pedantic, but Tess was engrossed.

They returned often. On their last visit, she tore a page out from her notebook and gave it to the man. Luke saw her do this, but he never asked her what that list was.

"You could just tell how much he loved his job," she said, "and his role there, preserving that past."

At her own job, Tess had moved to part-time. She was staying on to help train her replacement, a woman also named Tess, which seemed completely absurd.

"Capitalism," she said after the first day of this training. "She's nice. The new Tess. I've nicknamed her Healthy Tess and it's catching on. It's a good way to tell us apart."

"No, you didn't." He could hear the joke behind her voice, or else he hoped that he heard it.

"Okay, then I didn't." She shrugged. "Believe what you want."

Luke was glad to stay local for those first weeks because that was when his own work picked up.

The CMO had gotten back to him with more information at last. "The Fountain of Youth doohickey" had a real name: Prosyntus. Luke liked the sound of this. Prosyntus. It evoked old myths and legends, the winged horse Pegasus or Atlantis, the island lost under the sea.

A beloved singer had signed on to be their celebrity spokesperson. She'd be getting the procedure before it was widely released, and they could use her image in their early ads. Genesix had guidelines from a federal agency too. Specific language that Luke would have to incorporate. He'd have to categorize it as cosmetic. Apparently, there would otherwise have been a degree of social responsibility they'd need to uphold.

"And no one needs that," the CMO said.

"The end is near," Tess declared when Luke told her of these updates. "Good thing we have a procedure to make rich people look young forever."

This is it, he thought, gearing up to defend his career, his work, readying himself for a fight he'd long been waiting for.

"It also reduces pain?" he tried.

She laughed. "You know what else does that?" she said.

Luke thought, first, of the experimental drug Tess had turned down. But no, that wasn't what she was referring to. She meant that drug devastating what most people they knew would think was a smudge on the globe. The plant the drug came from: briar palm.

He didn't have it in him to defend his work after all. He only said, "I'm sorry, Tess," and he cut her off before she could say it: "And I know, my sorry does nothing to help."

He remembered the open graves in the photograph from Palmavja. He imagined Tess's future grave, which was just a pile of soil now. And he looked at her, because here she was, so furious at this world she would be leaving behind.

Terminally Ill Woman Rejects Xioneva Treatment, Chooses Death

IT MADE AN INTERESTING local headline for a time: Tess's rejection of a possible "cure." It was positioned as a counterpoint to the full-throated embrace of new science happening all around them.

Also she was young, beautiful, newly wed.

"So much life in her," the news anchors said, "and yet . . ."

This coverage tended not to mention the slim odds that Xioneva's treatment would give her even another two months or the much more probable side effects she'd encounter.

For a week, journalists came at them in public. There was a clamor of "Why?" and "How could you?" and "Don't."

"I'm not suicidal," she tried to explain to one especially dogged reporter. "I don't want to die. But I'm dying. It is only a matter of when."

It seemed practical, put that way.

One night, Tess and Luke watched a talk show called *Time Line* and there was a segment about Xioneva that mentioned Tess. It was bizarre. The host brought in an "expert" on Tess with bushy, crooked eyebrows whom Tess had never met.

It made Tess giddy each time they showed her picture on the television.

"The utter absurdity," she laughed.

She had told Luke that sometimes, she felt like she was seeing her life through the small end of a set of binoculars.

He pretended to understand what she meant by that.

Now though, Luke yelled at the screen. What did this expert know? What did anyone know?

"Fuck you," he said. "Leave her be."

Tess began laughing and could not stop for a minute.

"Aren't you angry?" Luke asked her.

"Why should I be?" she said. "You're mad enough for us both."

"Glad I could help," he said, and he shut it off.

They sat there in the darkness until Tess did stop laughing.

"You can be angry for yourself, you know," she said. "You don't have to just be angry for me."

I am, he thought. I am angry for myself, and angry with myself, and also, I am angry at you.

The fight might have finally happened then. But when he looked over at Tess again, her eyes were closed. She'd been having so much trouble sleeping lately. He let her rest her head against his shoulder and he didn't say anything else.

THE MORNING OF THE seizure, Luke had just submitted his final proposal for Prosyntus. He'd designed billboards downtown featuring headshots of celebrities who were scheduled to have the procedure. In each portrait, the very top of the face was obscured by a cloud. The year was printed in the corner. The image was stunning, strange, and persuasive. He'd fit the disclaimer language in small font at the very bottom. The company loved it. There was just one issue to address: the beloved singer dropped dead before recording her ads.

"But we've got it from here," the CMO told him. "We'll figure something out. Enjoy your vacation."

Enjoy your vacation. The phrase rang in Luke's head. He had told the CMO about Tess's condition, and why he was taking time off—so they could travel and complete her last wishes. There would be two international flights and, finally, the canyon. That would be it.

Then the seizure happened.

They had known she might start having seizures. And they knew that this would be a sign that she was nearing the end. Luke had specific instructions from the doctor to follow and he followed them. He timed how long the seizure lasted. He said what he was supposed to say, reminding her where she was and what had happened when her body stopped seizing and she tried to sit up.

But the way her eyes rolled around in her head and the jolts that her body made and how her face drained completely of blood. She looked hideous. Like the undead. He did not want to see her like that.

Maybe she should have taken the pills before the seizures started. That was another horrible thought that Plain Old Luke had.

It was becoming harder and harder to live with himself as he was getting ready to live without her.

There would be no international flights after all. The doctor had told them that if the seizures began, they should not fly.

Luke had to remind Tess of this, carefully. He didn't want to upset her if she'd forgotten.

"I have backups," she said.

"Backups?" he repeated.

"Easier things, closer. It's no surprise. The seizure. I mean, I am dying, right?"

"Right," he said, his tone heavy with sarcasm. "Right, right. You're dying. Silly of me to forget."

"Good one," she said.

The next day, Luke had no work to get to and he woke up late, feeling furious.

The end is near, he heard Tess's voice say. This was not supposed to be their future.

He biked to the back parking lot of Genesix. It abutted a forested stretch near the shore. He stayed there for hours, waiting, smelling the earthy, salty air, thinking about the future with Tess and the future without her and channeling all his anger into the glass-and-steel building where, thanks partly to him, rich people would soon have a cure for age. A cosmetic cure.

"You're still going to die," he said aloud because that was one thing he wished he had made more blatant in the branding. That Fountain of Youth doohickey—it didn't make you immortal. It froze you in time just as you were.

How did that help?

The sun was setting and he was cold and hungry and he needed to pee. He was still just as angry but he was unlocking his bike and was about to leave when the door opened and a woman wearing a white lab coat stepped out. She was smoking a cigarette.

"Hey!" he called.

She turned. She had a huge globe of hair and an ID card pinned to her coat.

On the card, there was a photo of her looking the way she looked right in front of him. Luke blinked and shook his head and tried to rid himself of the feeling that he was somewhere in a photo on a card pinned to a larger version of this same woman's coat. On and on and on like that.

"Dr. Wilhelm," he said, pulling himself back into this moment. That was what her name tag said: Dr. Naomi Wilhelm.

"And you are?" she asked, exhaling a thread of smoke.

"How does Prosyntus work?"

She was unfazed.

"And you are?" she repeated. She looked unhappy and exhausted. In small typeface beneath her name, he saw her title: senior researcher.

"What you are doing here"—he gestured toward the building—"how is it helping anyone?"

A beat.

"What publication do you work for?"

"I make ads," he said. "I made *your* ads." As if this helped explain anything, he added, "My wife is sick."

The woman said nothing.

"She's going to die," he said. "She's choosing to. It's like"—his voice cracked—"she's leaving me."

There, he thought, let this woman see how ugly Plain Old Luke was. He began to weep and he did not try to hide it. He waited for her to respond to his awfulness.

The woman kept smoking but something like contempt curled her lip as she watched him, crying messily and feeling sorry for himself.

When she finished smoking, she stared at him meanly, eyes squinting, before she stomped out her cigarette and went back inside.

Luke stayed there for a long while, weeping, hating the woman, the work he had done for her, hating her company, hating himself.

TESS WAS CLOSELY MONITORED for four weeks and there was no second seizure. For no clear reason, her condition plateaued. They had a few good months, which was unbelievable. Then a few more. A whole year. They knew this was stolen time they were not supposed to have. She would still die, of course, just not as soon as everyone thought.

She began taking long walks on the weekends alone, and the mere fact of that—Tess feeling well enough to take long walks alone—helped Luke to unwrap some layers of bitterness he'd let accumulate around him. His urge to scream at the world with Tess still in it subsided. He went back to work, took on new clients.

One Sunday, he caught up to Tess when she was taking a walk. He was planning to surprise her and take her out for brunch at a diner.

She didn't see him. She was near the gate of the large cemetery that was also an arboretum. The leaves were vibrant, cascading around her.

There was a child with her. A girl wearing a bright blue baseball cap.

The two were deep in a conversation that Luke could not hear. He watched them and he had the thought that if—somehow—things stayed the way they were now, they might still have a child one day. He thought of Tess as a mother, and he snapped a photograph—her and the girl on that bench. It became one of his very favorite pictures. He never showed it to Tess, and he left without her seeing him.

Later that same summer, things took a turn and she worsened.

He used the last week of his paid time off for the year. They set out to take their long road trip and finish The List.

So here it was at last: the canyon.

"Here it is," they said at the same time.

It was both like and unlike what he'd expected it to be. A piece of him had maybe thought of it, all along, as a place they'd ascend to. After all, they had kind of been building up to it, making their way through The List. Luke had imagined, dumbly, that there would be a way to see the whole thing as if from very high up. But you can never see the whole of anything you're still inside of.

At the east viewpoint, they met a blind man. He had a guide dog and he let them pet her.

The man told them that he came to the canyon to breathe in the air. They breathed it in, the three of them and the dog.

It was a great place to take a photograph but Luke could not take a photograph because he had no more film, so instead, he just blinked slowly and pretended his eyes were a camera shutter clicking closed.

They stayed like that. Breathing. Luke decided that the air wasn't any different. But the breathing might be. That if you let it, the breathing could be different each time.

"What do you see?" the man asked after a while.

They were quiet, considering.

Luke said, "I can see these signs of time having passed that usually I can't see."

"How so?" the man asked.

"Like how a river can cut through rock if you give it long enough. I think I knew that, but I couldn't imagine it until now."

Luke had overheard a guide tell a tour group that two tiny sediments in one stripe of color could have been laid down when different life forms were roaming the planet. That got him worked up, thinking of time at such massive quantities within something so small.

"And what do you see?" the man said to Tess. She was turned with her back to the canyon.

"You know," she said, "I always thought it would be this great wonder of emptiness." She stared at Luke. "But now that I'm here, it really doesn't look empty at all."

A SET OF IMAGES Luke would not remember: Tess wearing a plastic wristband and a white gown of paper. Tess sleeping in a robotic bed and eating meals off a tray table. A small screen playing snow in the corner. Their every conversation punctured by the beeps of machines that kept her and others like her alive. Endless interruptions by knocks on a door and a person with cold, gloved hands who needed to touch her body and collect data about what her body was doing.

This was not how it happened, so he could neither forget nor remember it this way. He was grateful for that.

So how did it happen?

They returned home.

Luke had never imagined they would have this much time: Plain Old Luke and Dying Tess. But this was it now: the end.

One night they were reading one of her notebooks of lists together, reminiscing, when Luke got to the list of ominous headlines. The names "Genesix" and "Prosyntus" jumped out at him several times.

She had been following news of the procedure even after his work on the project ended.

"It's creepy," she said and shrugged.

Toward the bottom, a headline:

Dr. Naomi Wilhelm, Researcher at Genesix, Dead in Apparent Suicide

Naomi Wilhelm. Luke remembered her and that strange night they met.

Why did he feel like the victim of every interaction?

He thought, I have only been the witness to someone else's great tragedy.

Tess had another seizure and a third and a fourth soon after. There would be no fifth. They both knew. There was a farewell dinner with her family and friends, and then it was the two of them. Just as she wanted, and just as she planned. He watched her swallow the pills and he sat on the bed beside her.

What were they supposed to say to each other?

"What are we supposed to say to each other?" Tess asked.

Luke said, "You've gotten really good, you know, at reading my mind."

AT THE CANYON, AT one point, the blind man had scratched his dog's ears and said, "I don't know what I'll do without her." Luke realized that the man was young, maybe thirty-five. But his guide dog was old; her once-gold hair was almost all white.

Luke had waited for Tess to say it. It was the perfect moment to explain. But Tess said nothing.

Why didn't he say it himself? It could have been simple. He might have just said, "Me either."

On the long drive back from the canyon, Tess kept falling asleep in the car. The List was complete and Luke talked to her as he drove because, even though she was sleeping, she was still with him.

SHE WAS NOT ASLEEP yet, but she would be soon.

THEY HAD DRIVEN PAST a Prosyntus billboard, his own design. He thought about the procedure. What if he had it? Not right now, but later. What if he had Prosyntus once he was alone?

"What if I had it?" he said. "Prosyntus?"

"Not because I'm vain," he explained to her silence.

In his memory, Tess would stay the way she was now forever. He didn't want to be the one to keep changing. It was selfish, he knew. Still.

Could she understand that?

"Can you understand that?" he asked.

She began grinding her teeth in her sleep, and the noise was almost seismic. Why couldn't you capture a sound in a photograph?

He told her, "I know my pain is small in comparison, but it's all that I have." And could she understand *that*?

That was the last question he'd asked before she woke up.

Because then she woke up.

But now, she would not.

Nonetheless, he asked it again.

In the car, his mouth had been dry from talking and his muscles were tired and the highway was clogging with traffic of all the people who were out doing all the things that they did or did not have written down on lists somewhere.

When Tess woke up, she held his hand. He felt a weight from it, a heaviness, pressing into his palm from hers. He didn't know what the weight was at the time, but he knew he would go on feeling it long afterward, and maybe forever.

Now, as he watched her sleeping, he realized what that weight was and he told her.

This was the last thing he'd say to Tess.

He told her: It is the weight of something you thought would be empty, but which you find instead is utterly full.

OMINOUS HEADLINES

Extinct Animal Cloned

The Next 'Big One': Is Marks Island Overdue for Seismic Disaster?

VextaGen's Technology Assists in First Human Head Transplant

Genesix Says Age Is '100% Preventable'

Famous Woolly Mammoth Clone Dies

Genesix: Prophylactic for Age Will Also Block Chronic Pain

Xioneva Experimental Cancer Drug Extends
Life by One to Two Months

Monique Gray, the Performance Artist Everyone Wants a Piece Of

Genesix Shifts Tone with 'Purely Cosmetic' Antiaging Procedure

The Pandemic of Forgetting: Once Rare,
Early Dementia Increasingly Common

Terminally Ill Woman Rejects Xioneva Treatment, Chooses Death

Exclusive! Artist Monique Gray's Harrowing Past

Alfred Siegler, Biotech Mogul, Pleads Guilty
for Role in Palmavja Drug Crisis

First Human Head Transplant Recipient, 44, Dead

Toxic Algae Bloom Closes Resident Beach, Baffles Scientists

Dr. Naomi Wilhelm, Researcher at Genesix,
Dead in Apparent Suicide

–5–

A QUARTER CENTURY OF SLEEP

IT WAS DIFFICULT TO MOVE HER INTO THE CAVES, requiring an air-conditioned trailer towed by ambulance, a crane to lift and lower her along with her special bed. He thinks of her in those caves now, sleeping.

Until today, she was in the same house, in the same room, and in the same bed for twenty-five years. But how fitting it had felt when Mr. Marks proposed that they take her here to his museum. How he'd expected—

What? What did you expect to happen, Lionel? That you'd reunite with Evangeline?

That's his late wife's voice in his head. He still hears her sometimes but less and less often.

He watches the audience. The Congregants' orange robes make them stand out. Even during the years of their worship, he never allowed them to tend to his daughter or even to touch her. He cared for her all by himself. He was a good father in that way.

Though in other ways, you really weren't.

There are many unfamiliar faces around him: a pregnant woman wearing all black, a middle-aged couple with similar haircuts, a scared-looking woman half-hidden behind a pillar, and then, there—

Are those the old neighbors?

Yes, he sees several families from Jacob's Circle seated toward the back. He feels almost tickled by their boldness, their hypocrisy. What would his late wife say if she were here to see them?

What would you say, Naomi?

He waits for her to say something, but she will never answer his direct questions.

"It's criminal," these same neighbors wrote in their official complaint to the community board, "what's being done to his child." They cited the crowds of "fanatics" on the front lawn, the fact that he'd installed a picture window in his daughter's bedroom. "Exploitative," they called it.

He tries to make eye contact with them, but not a single one will glance at him.

Another face jumps out at him. His wife's old boss, Dr. Dean.

Why is he here?

Time has been unkind to him. The skin on his face looks loose, like a mask.

–6–

Ten months before Maeve's sleep

HIS DAUGHTERS WERE VERY QUIET. LIONEL KEPT TURNING to the back seat, making sure they were still there, still buckled. He spoke to fill the silence. He told them about the first Halloween that he had spent with Naomi. The two of them were going to a costume party. They were new to their jobs and had no extra money for a costume they'd wear only once. So their mother had bought just one thing: a roll of white duct tape. They'd cut out all the bones in the human body from that tape and stuck them onto black shirts and black pants.

"We made terrific skeletons."

He turned right and stopped at a light.

They were headed to a costume store, which was why he'd brought up this story, but now he was imagining his dead wife as a skeleton. He tried to stop imagining it, but he could think of nothing else. She'd been dead for four months.

How long, he wondered, did it take the human body to decompose?

"What about the back?" Evangeline asked. Or it could have been Maeve. He never could tell their voices apart without looking at them.

"What?" he said.

"The backs of your costumes. Did they have bones too?"

That was a good question. He couldn't say how they had done it. Maybe they'd stood with their backs against the wall the whole party. That seemed possible.

"I don't remember," he said. A grief overcame him at this small, lost memory.

He told himself to focus on what he did remember. It had taken a lot longer than he'd expected, cutting all those bones out of white tape.

He remembered being surprised at just how many distinct bones the human body was filled with. He remembered saying something like that to Naomi and Naomi staring at him and squinting as she corrected him.

"A body isn't *filled* with bones, Lionel. The bones *are* your body."

Had she seemed particularly unhappy?

The detectives had asked him that the morning after a fisherman had found her body.

No, he'd said, because she hadn't. Not *particularly*.

Their second Halloween together, Lionel remembered, he had found a cheap beetle costume at a yard sale. He wore it for the next three years straight. What had happened to it? He especially liked the exoskeleton, a hard, iridescent layer worn on the outside, which—for a beetle—was where it belonged.

This year, what would he dress as? He thought about wearing a box. Dressing not as the insect but as the thought experiment: the beetle in the box. Who would understand that? Naomi would have because he'd told her of it on an early date. All those thought experiments he loved to think about.

Naomi used to handle the girls' costumes, and he didn't know how she came up with the ideas or made the girls go along with them. There were a lot of these everyday riddles he had to go about solving now.

"What if you go as one thing together?" he suggested to his daughters as the idea occurred to him. "Like a horse or a donkey or zebra? One of you can be the front half, and the other the back."

It would be easy to keep track of them that way. Plus, one costume would be cheaper than two. It was a great idea. "Won't that be fun?"

"How would we walk upstairs?" the girls asked.

"Ah." Another good question. "Right."

So, what now, Naomi? he asked in his head. Sometimes he heard her voice, but right now, his late wife said nothing.

Lionel had shaved off his mustache long ago, before his wedding, but since Naomi's death, he had been feeling the ghost of it hovering over his lip. As if being a widower returned him to bachelorhood. He touched it, the phantom mustache, in that bald spot below his nose.

"What will you be then?" he asked the girls, pulling into a parking spot. He forced some spirit into his voice. "It's Halloween! You can be whatever you want."

The girls had seen, in the car mirror, how their father's face fell when they rejected his one suggestion. They felt a twinge of guilt. His best ideas never panned out.

It had been a tough time for him. For all of them. Their mother had died that summer and their father wasn't back to his old self. They didn't know if he would be. They weren't back to their old selves either, they could tell. But they were kids and they were still growing so they were changing all the time. There were lots and lots of things they never knew could happen until they happened. Like it could *hail*, which basically meant that icy rocks fell from the sky. A parent could die. You could murder your own self—there was even a word for that. They'd learned that word too: "suicide."

Each twin had made the private decision not to be matching. They'd been matching every Halloween before in costumes their mother had made. They longed to be something—anything—of their own.

Neither twin had told her sister about the vow she had made with herself, so it became a waiting game. She could not choose a costume until her sister did. But, of course, her sister could not choose a costume either. And so, they were stuck.

This was how they figured out what the other was up to, and even this private pact became something they shared.

It was what their father would call a paradox. Like the twin paradox, which they still did not understand, though they'd heard him explain it a thousand times by now. Somehow one twin ended up being both younger and older than the other? Anyway, being twins had lots of paradoxes.

They unbuckled their seat belts and got out of the car.

Hall of Hauntings was open all year. The adult costumes were horribly gruesome. Bloody werewolves, bloody doctors, bloody brides. There was blood everywhere and a million body parts. Swollen lips, bulging eyeballs, hairy man legs. It wasn't the most kid-friendly store. Lionel had forgotten this.

"Let's stick together," he said. "I'll grab mine first."

This year, he'd decided he'd be a cow. It was the subtle gender swapping of it that was fun. He'd have udders and fake eyelashes. It would be almost like dressing up as a lady. That was what was great about Halloween. On a normal day, he had no desire to dress this way. But he could on Halloween, so he figured, Why not?

"Wait here," he said as he went into the dressing room. He put on the cow suit quickly and came out to show them. He stared at himself for a minute, loving it. A cow was such a majestic, maternal creature.

"Girls," he said. But his girls were not in the reflection.

"Shit," he said. Then, "Sorry," to apologize to them for the swear.

But no, his girls were nowhere behind him. His tail swept against the dirty floor as he walked and then ran down the aisles.

"Girls?" he said, shouting. "Girls!"

Silently, the girls walked away from their father and away from each other. Each parted her own path through the wigs and the face paints, passing a dress made of doll heads, a clown with yellow teeth and bloodshot eyes. They wondered about this holiday. Why did adults return to these childish things? The dress looked heavy. And all those doll heads would bang together whenever you walked. There was something about the clown's smile that looked like their father. They hated that they thought that. But they did. The baby section was similarly confounding. Babies as lobsters being cooked in pots. A baby as what looked like a homeless man. A baby with a lump of poop it could wear on its head. Humiliating.

One sister strolled slowly with a hand out, touching every costume she passed. She'd stop to consider an option before finding its flaw. She could be a shark but it was boyish, a cat but it was boring, a giraffe but it was a ridiculous construction; her own face would peek out from the base of its neck.

The other sister walked more deliberately. She kept thinking she knew what she wanted. She'd eye a section and rush toward it, stop, consider a costume and know that no, she was wrong. Even when she did find what she'd been looking for, the reality of it wasn't what she had pictured. She rejected a watermelon, a vampire, a pilot.

When Lionel found them, they were inside costumes that they'd tried on over their clothes: a hot dog and an elderly man.

"I couldn't find you," he said, breathless. "Do you know how scared I was?"

One daughter was blanketed by a hot dog bun. The other had a bald cap and a cane. They were safe, his daughters.

He saw them, all three, reflected in a mirror at the end of the aisle: a cow, a hot dog, a shrunken old man. He didn't know who was in which costume, but it didn't matter.

The old man's wire glasses slipped down her nose. He put a hand around each of their heads and pulled them into his shoulders. The hot dog smelled slightly of relish.

"Okay," he whispered. "Okay," he said, crying softly behind his cow mask. "You're okay. We're okay. We're okay."

Their father paid for their costumes and they left, still wearing them. The girls didn't know why he had cried like that. His eyelashes, as a cow, looked longer. Didn't they? And they felt a little afraid of his udders—why? They kept thinking about it as they drove home. How, when he had bent down to hold them, his udders had been right there, rubbery, hollow.

They thought of their mother and how she would never have let their father dress in a cow suit. They knew this, but they could not have said why.

They tried to feel good that they had done what they came for. They had found something different to be for a while. This was what it felt like, they told themselves, looking at each other look different. But they knew that inside their separate costumes, everything was still the same. They didn't feel any different, anyway.

Their father parked the car and unlocked the side door of the house from the garage.

Inside, they each stood in front of a different closet mirror. They peeled off one set of clothing, and they put on the next.

—

ALL WINTER, THE HARBOR was empty. When spring came, the fishing boats appeared again, like birds flying home from the south. The girls would fall asleep with a certain number of boats on the horizon, and when they woke up, there would be more. It didn't matter how early they woke up. The boats beat them. They used to count these boats with their mother at Rocky Beach, but they had never considered the fishermen who brought the boats there, undetected, every night.

"No one sees the fishermen," their father said.

"Why not?" they asked.

"Fishermen are like the tooth fairy," he said simply.

Their father was teasing them, they knew. He was getting back to himself, slowly. Although he was still—what was the right word? Was there a word that meant both dreamy and sad?

By the start of the summer, the horizon was dotted with boats everywhere, bobbing and facing up the hill toward their yard. Their father liked the view of them. "Like a postcard," he said.

Despite themselves, the girls came to fear the fishermen. It was a small fear, but it was constant. The boats seemed to stare right at them. The girls could easily imagine the whole fleet freeing themselves from their buoys and washing up the hill onto their lawn, the ghostly fishermen stepping out of those boats and saying in one deep voice, "Here we are. We're the Fishermen, and we're here."

Also, there was how their mother used to love counting the boats and then she had disappeared into the harbor along with them.

The girls had seen their mother the night that it happened. This was a secret they never talked about. But they'd watched from the window as she swam out into the ocean. After that, they never saw her again.

So any one of the fishermen could have been the one to find her. Or maybe a fisherman killed her? Nobody had explained to them how it had really happened. They both wanted and did not want to know.

"Why do boats need names?" his daughters had asked.

"For a fisherman," he'd said, "a boat's like a pet."

Some boats had joke names. *Midlife Crisis* was Lionel's favorite. The girls preferred the boats with names like people. *Kevin* appeared late in the season and was gone for a weekend before he returned.

"*Kevin* is back!" they yelled. "Did you say hello to *Kevin*?"

"Hello, *Kevin*," he said stiffly, which made the girls giggle. He sometimes had the sense that they were humoring him.

Kevin was a very plain boat. Lionel had once looked up "boat" in the girls' illustrated dictionary and the picture looked exactly like *Kevin*. He took the page to them and showed them the resemblance.

"No," they said, becoming hysterical. "That doesn't look like *Kevin* at all."

Why was that so funny?

He didn't know but he laughed too, so maybe he was the one humoring them? Maybe they all humored each other. Maybe that was all a family was, in the end.

The girls liked *Kevin*, but there was a boat they liked even better: *Fish Magnet*. That one was hilarious. They could not even properly be afraid of the fisherman who owned it. In some moods, they couldn't even say the name *Fish Magnet* without erupting into laughter and spit.

"*Fish Magnet*!" one sister yelled as she ran back and forth through the sprinkler. It was completely random.

"*Fish Magnet*!" her sister echoed, taking her turn. She had recently started copying everything her sister did. She had given up any attempt to be different. It never worked. Not really. They would always be identical.

They walked away from the sprinkler and went to the fence so they could gaze out at her. There she was, moving up and down, gently.

"*Fish Magnet*," one sister whispered.

It never got old.

The sea around her glistened, as if winking at them. They thought of their mother and they fell silent. Things were funny until they weren't anymore.

The day she died, they awoke to the small noise of their mother's footsteps in the kitchen. They got out of bed without saying anything and sat at the top of the stairs. It wasn't yet morning. She was wearing a bathing suit that had pants and looked like it was made of sealskin. Why? She drank a glass of tap water and some cold coffee from a jar she kept in the refrigerator. They did not think she knew they were there, watching her, but right before she walked out the front door, she turned around. She waved up the stairs at them. They waved back. She put a finger to her lips and nodded.

Quiet, she was telling them. They made the same gesture and nodded back. *We will be quiet*, they meant. She blew them a kiss. Just one kiss. They were meant to share it.

THE BLOOM WAS ALL anyone in Jacob's Circle could talk about that summer. That and the weather. The heat wave, which kept climbing, unbroken, and then the ocean at the beach club, topped with an unappealing film of algae.

The bloom had begun the previous summer, a neighbor learned, but it had been limited to Marks Island proper. This year it had spread and grown worse. It had been triggered by something new introduced to the waters, probably. It wasn't toxic, this neighbor said. But to be safe, the beach at Jacob's Circle was closed.

The algae was red and leafy and it twinkled at night. The grown-ups had never seen anything like it. No other local beaches were experiencing it. The way the current flowed, it was all being washed up directly from Grace Beach on Marks Island to them on their quiet cul-de-sac.

Lucky us, the grown-ups said, rolling their eyes at one another.

Through the crest of the heat wave, there was the look of the algae bloom out there; curdling and unrelenting, a sludge.

The neighbors of Jacob's Circle had to content themselves on Saturdays and Sundays with stretching out not on the sand but at the pool.

Families left their pails and shovels in the garage. They purchased pool toys and got used to the scent of chlorine in their hair and in their laundry hampers.

The kids pushed their inflatable armbands up to their biceps so that the pointy corners pinched into their armpits. The grown-ups hated the noise this made, the terrible squeak of plastic on skin. Like balloons rubbing together. Why did festive things give them the chills?

Each family came with a cooler filled with ice packs, juice boxes, string cheese, sliced carrots or apples, and three or four fish sandwiches. There was universal dislike of crusts among the children, so crusts were done away with. Bodies were painted with sunscreen not fully rubbed in. And the heat and the bloom. It was a nightmarish combination.

If it rained, they would remain poolside. If it thundered, they would pack up and leave. They decided this once and never had to return to the decision. It did not thunder. It did not rain. Nonetheless, they became a poolside community in that moment, for they had made decisions about rules together.

The grown-ups took turns carrying kids on their shoulders while swimming, holding babies in the baby pool, dipping their feet before lifting them high.

At their private beach, the algae kept blooming. In the sky, the clouds kept not raining. At the pool, the grown-ups gave each other nicknames that did not fit them. KelKel, Mimi, Bob-O, Skip.

Skip was the third nickname they had tried on the man. The first names they came up with for him hadn't stuck.

"Could he be Nell?" someone asked. No, he could not be. That was a woman's name. "How about just one letter: L?" This didn't work either, too slight. Someone said, "Lion?" and everyone laughed. At last, the name Skip was suggested. They were all grateful for that even though Skip bore no relation to his real name. He just maybe looked a bit like that old musician.

"You know," Skip said thoughtlessly, "no one has called me Skip before."

Actually, someone had called him Skip. She had said it only once, long ago. He remembered this later, lying out on a pool chair, the memory nagging at the base of his skull—why had she called him that? He stood and immersed his feet in the water, and when the memory slipped away again, it was forgotten completely. This time, perhaps for good.

Skip was a widower. His wife had died at the start of the previous summer. Everyone remembered, but danced around mentioning her. He was an entomologist, they learned, and he owned all kinds of rare bugs. They asked him what he thought of the algae bloom.

"I'm just a bug guy," he said, unhelpfully. "Not a fun-gi." He laughed at himself. Then he added, "I'm kidding. Algae is not a fungus."

"Oh?" they said, not listening.

And that got him going. His late wife might have known, he said. She had studied the ancient Marks Island ecosystem and even published some breakthrough research about it. She might have understood the cause of this algae out there.

They'd walked right into that, unwittingly. The late wife.

But yes, he went on, he was a bug guy, and they should all bring their kids to his museum and soon because his larvae had pupated.

"We will," they told him. But they would not.

His daughters, the twins, they seemed normal. But they acted odd. Or one did. She had begun shadowing her sister, following her and mimicking everything that she did. The other girl never noticed or pretended not to. She didn't acknowledge this identical person who took an identical towel and wrapped it around herself in the identical way. It was an uncanny scene to behold. Like she had an imaginary friend everybody could see. And it was only one of them who followed the other, right? Or did they sometimes take turns?

When the sun set, a grown-up would appear with a box of popsicles from the snack bar. The kids who came first could pick their colors. Sadly, there were never enough blues.

"Don't run!" the grown-ups said. "Slow!"

After that, there was no more swimming. The children dripped sugar water onto the pool deck, and the grown-ups talked about summers past when the children were younger and when the babies were no one at all. If there were any sandwiches left, they were divided. The children's lips and tongues were painted green and orange and red and the coveted blue.

The pool chairs were typical pool chairs. They had adjustable backs and three-inch-wide slats of plastic running horizontally across them. The children played with these slats as they licked their popsicles. They twisted them around and leaned into them to impress marks on their bodies. They traced the imprints of those strips on one another and came to know the feeling of each other's fingers in the marks on their skin.

There were many children. Almost a classroom full. And so near in age they had to measure it in quarter years to tell who was really the oldest. There was a clear tallest. She was the tallest by several inches. And the shortest—was there something wrong with him? Why was he so small?

The adults could lose track of the children for an entire half hour, guessing they were just in the back of the beach club or else on the grassy patch that they called "the park." Nobody noticed that they went down to the ocean, which was supposed to be closed now. Nobody saw the games the children played with that red seaweed that had begun washing up everywhere. They chased each other around with it. They wrapped it over their wrists as bracelets or around each other's necks. They pretended to eat it. "Pretended" being the operative word—except they may have tricked one of the twins into eating it. They never told her it was a joke so they could keep playing the same prank on her. She ate so much of it.

They all ran back to the pool when the popsicles arrived and they were yelled at for running, but nothing else. The seaweed games were a shared secret that summer.

Every day at the beach club ended this same way.

The hot air, heavy and humid, the pool still and empty, the frozen water on sticks bleeding drop by drop onto the grateful ants below. One hundred feet away the waves came in with the algae and the waves rolled out, but the algae remained.

–7–

A QUARTER CENTURY OF SLEEP

THE CAR IS A RENTAL SHE GOT FROM THE AIRPORT, AND nothing is where she expects it to be. Crossing the isthmus, she tries to lower her window but ends up almost opening the trunk by mistake. She wants to breathe in the scent of the ocean. She lives far from the sea on purpose, but she misses the smell of it.

A sign welcomes her to ancient Marks Island and an old nursery rhyme surfaces in her mind.

Have you been to Marks? (Yes, ma'am.)

How did you get to Marks? (I swam.)

Twenty-five years, she thinks. That's the gap between her and her own identical twin. It sounds like one of her father's old thought experiments. How could someone be older than her own twin?

Years ago, she gave up trying to solve all the riddles of her family. She chose to accept that hers might not be a unique experience; there are puzzles in everyone's childhood they expect will make sense once they get older.

Her grandfather's advice: "It's like a scab. If you keep scratching for answers, it scars."

This was back when she was a teenager, waiting for a response to a letter. She'd check the mail first thing when she got home from school. Pace by the mailbox on Saturdays, hoping for answers.

"To heal," her grandfather said, "you have to learn to live with the itch."

So she learned to live with it.

About a month ago, her grandfather called. "A piece of mail came for you."

"It's probably junk," she said. "You can throw it out." Nothing important was sent for her at her grandfather's address anymore.

"It's from your father," he said.

"Oh." She gathered herself, said, joking, "Right, junk. You can throw it out."

"Too late," her grandfather said. He'd already sent it to her first class. The invitation for the ceremony arrived the following day.

THE CEREMONY WILL START in another minute. She gets to the main parking lot, but it is full. An attendant in a reflective vest directs her to a spillover lot on a grassy stretch beside Grace Beach.

She should hurry. She will miss the welcome remarks, and she doesn't want to draw attention to herself when she comes in.

THE INVITATION LOOKED MORE like a promotional flyer. It was printed on cheap newsprint that would turn to pulp if it got the slightest bit wet. There was no personal message, no hint as to why he was reaching out to her.

It said the ceremony would be at the Marks Museum of Human History. The museum owner would host it. Tickets could be purchased in advance or, for an added fee, day of at the door.

Those in attendance could create an Archive of Sleep. They could bring any object they wanted to offer for Maeve to remember.

It said Maeve would be moved into the Caves of Adina.

The Caves of Adina? she thought when she read that. Why?

SHE GETS OUT OF the car, puts on her jacket.

Across the water, there's the planned community of Jacob's Circle. She squints one eye to make her perspective warp and points so that her index finger appears giant. Right before making contact, she brings her thumb up and squeezes, pinching her old home into a grain of sand.

There's the harbor of Rocky Beach too, with its fishing boats. The names on those boats are only blurs she cannot decipher. She used to love the boat names, but both in her vision and in her recollection, the names are too far away to see.

Time to go, she thinks, and she wills herself to head to the entrance before she misses everything.

AFTER RECEIVING THE INVITATION, she did more research. She learned that the Marks Museum had barely managed to stay afloat all these years. The owner had to sell off much of the collection.

The last event at his museum was a gala for the city.

She found a photo from the gala. In it, the museum owner was standing with her mother's former boss at Genesix: Dr. Gregory Dean.

She stared at that photograph for a full minute.

Dr. Dean had one large arm around the other man's shoulders in a firm embrace. He smiled with his teeth parted as though, in another moment, he'd laugh.

Why would the two of them have been so chummy?

For the millionth time, she thought of the rocks—those shimmering red rocks that her mother was always looking for, the red rocks that were found on her body, the red rocks that were part of an artifact, a doll discovered inside the caves. There had to be a connection.

Somebody must know something.

As she thought this, her hand curled into a claw. Overtaken by a tremendous itch, she scratched at her forearm until she drew blood.

-8-

Twenty-one months into Maeve's sleep

A MEMORY: ABE MAKING SYL GUESS THE NEXT CELEBrity patient. "Who will it be?" he pressed her. "Let's bet a dollar on it."

They were talking of Prosyntus. Celebrities were demanding it in a rush. At first, it was mostly old actors whose names were already slipping to the tips of tongues. But then even those who were more freshly famous began having the procedure.

Here was Syl struggling to come up with a likely candidate. "Monique Gray?" she guessed. As soon as she said it, she knew it was wrong. But why exactly?

"Who's Monique Gray?" That was J. P., wanting to play the game with his parents.

"Monique Gray?" Abe spoke gently. "The performance artist? Remember, she came out with that statement condemning Prosyntus last week?"

SYL WAS EATING BREAKFAST at the kitchen counter. J. P. was between her and Abe. The morning news was on their small TV above the fridge, and an ad for Prosyntus played during each commercial break. They ate without speaking.

Syl had hated the name "Prosyntus" since the beginning. It made the procedure sound sterile and mythological while giving no clue as to what it really entailed. Medical language was like that. It hid its meaning, withheld what it could do. She and Abe had been calling it "The Process," but this was misleading as well. Prosyntus stopped a process; it didn't make one begin.

For a time, Prosyntus maintained its celebrity status. It was constant and yet removed from their normal existence. After the old actors, the supermodels lined up to preserve their bodies at the peaks of their careers. Athletes came next, though the ethical questions about that remained. Questions like, Should there be forced retirement for athletes who'd had the procedure? If so, when?

Now, it was something anyone could have if they chose to. Syl tried to see why anyone would choose to. She pictured a future where she approached death without any physical signs of aging, without changing. It was a hard image to hold on to. Her hair started sprouting curly white wires, like springs loosened from a clock. Her spine bent into a question mark.

This was how memory distorted imagination. It was impossible to empty the future of the past it was meant to contain.

After breakfast J. P. reminded his parents that his class was taking a field trip later that week. The end-of-year trip to Marks Island. Syl would be chaperoning.

"I think you'll go into the Caves of Adina this time," Abe said.

J. P.'s eyes widened. "What's that?"

"I don't want to ruin the surprise," Abe said. "You'll see."

J. P. looked at Syl, anxious, and she patted his leg. "They aren't scary," she said. "You'll like them."

J. P. was not his father. Syl would have liked to remind Abe of this for the hundredth time. He was not the way Abe was when Abe was a boy. Not that Syl had known Abe then. But she'd heard his stories. Young Abe, an intrepid little explorer, hiking around Marks Island on his own.

Abe would climb into the Caves of Adina and through the passage that led to what had once been a shore. He would stand out there and pretend he was one of the ancient people who'd made that place home. It was all new—newly old, that was, freshly discovered.

J. P. was sensitive and nervous by nature. Thoughtful and curious, like his father, but more of a worrier than his father had been.

Outside, a car beeped. It was J. P.'s ride to school, Evangeline and her grandfather. J. P. hopped off the stool, kissed his parents, grabbed his lunch from the counter, and left.

Syl was brushing her teeth when Abe told her he'd be having The Process. It wasn't the first time he'd said it. The first time he said it, she was stunned into silence. And the second time, she decided Abe was kidding. He had to be. She jutted her chin and teased him.

"Okay," she said, "maybe there's a two-for-one discount. We can both have it. Maybe J. P. should have it too."

The procedure was not approved for use on children. They both knew this much, even though most details about Prosyntus were not yet disclosed.

"You're joking," Abe replied. "But I'm not."

He had made his first appointment and he spoke of logistics. When it was over, would Syl be able to meet him at the facility? It was scheduled for Friday. From then on, it would be monthly injections. Someone would need to sign for him this first time, to drive him home. Could she do that?

Syl wanted to protest. To scream. To throw a tantrum. To make it stop. But it was too late. Abe had made up his mind, like crossing a threshold. Their reflections caught eyes in the bathroom mirror.

Yes, she told Abe, she could.

It was Syl's turn to make dinner. J. P. was helping roll out the pizza dough. He dipped his hands into a bag of flour. When he pulled them out, they were the hands of a ghost. Syl needed to tell him about his father. She didn't want to, but she should. Their son deserved to know.

She could start with, "It is a choice your father has made for his body." Or, "It has nothing to do with you or with me." Neutral, journalistic language. The problem was that it should have everything to do with them. Shouldn't it? And then again, maybe it did.

She chopped vegetables and J. P. arranged them on the pizza, making a face with mushroom eyes. He was so young. His family must still seem like an extension of his body, his self. He hadn't yet realized that this life was in no way inevitable. Parents, for instance. Most parents did not have such a wide gap of time between them.

Abe was older than Syl by twenty-three years. It was a long time, longer than the life span of a family pet. J. P. did not yet see this gap or how it formed a fault line between his mother and father. But one day he would. Syl expected J. P. to ask over his cornflakes any morning why Evangeline's grandfather was about the same age as his dad.

"Mom," J. P. said. He was setting the table. "Wednesday's the field trip. Please don't forget."

Had she forgotten?

Yes. Once. Twice. She made a note and taped it to the cabinet. Just two words: "Don't forget."

"IT DOES NOT POSTPONE death. Remember that," the artist was saying. She was being interviewed for a talk show called *Time Line* at the news station where Syl worked.

Syl could see several images of the artist at the same time. One was real—she was small and faced forward; the others were projected and enlarged from so many angles on so many screens. One camera zoomed in on Monique Gray's face, and the beauty mark beside her lips was rendered in full, three-dimensional detail.

Syl thought the words "beauty mark" as she stared at it. A euphemism for what it really was: a mole. An ugly one, too, on an otherwise gorgeous woman. Gray was young. She had risen to fame from seemingly nowhere earlier that year. She had come out as the strongest voice against Prosyntus.

"You are fooling yourselves," Gray pronounced. "This procedure—it's a curse. No matter how many superficial attempts we make to cheat pain and death, it doesn't matter: pain and death always win."

This was more than Gray had said publicly. She was an artist who had been known as much for her gruesome and esoteric art as she was for her silence about it.

Syl had no interest in celebrity culture, but she knew about Gray because everyone had come to know about Gray. Also it had been a reporter at Syl's own news station who had broken the story. The reporter was an obnoxious woman. She fancied herself an investigative journalist, but Syl could recall the early days of the reporter's career when she had written nonsense—overeager fluff pieces, listicles, features with no hard news angle, five hundred words to accompany an interesting photograph of a blue whale. Just that kind of thing for years. Later, celebrity gossip disguised as cultural criticism.

And now she'd broken the story of how Gray had come to Marks Island City as a refugee, hidden her past, and changed her name.

Syl felt sad for Monique Gray, who sat on the orange couch under studio lighting taking a faux stand, Syl assumed, against The Process. It seemed like a weak attempt to wrest back control of her narrative.

The host asked Gray about the billboards on the highway.

"Those?" Gray said. "Yes, I've seen them. They fill the air like locusts."

On each, there was a portrait of a beautiful celebrity who'd had The Process. Their features were so symmetrical they looked alien, and their foreheads disappeared into clouds. Strange advertising. But memorable. Gripping.

"We need to remember," Gray said, "Prosyntus has not made these people beautiful. Fame and money have done that. We forget this. Although yes, it's true, Prosyntus will keep them there. They won't age."

On the billboards, there was the catchphrase: "Make age just a number."

"I get it," she said. "It's persuasive."

The host nodded.

"But it's not magic. It isn't even medicine. It blocks aging, numbs pain. It stops symptoms so maybe you can forget about death for a while, but death will happen. One day, you—like everyone else—will be dead."

Gray stopped, breathless, letting that sink in. The statement carried a subtext of what everyone had learned about her and the depths of her grief.

The host turned to the camera with a big-toothed grin. "Stay with us," she said. "*Time Line* will be right back."

Syl left the set to head to her office. It would be difficult to fact-check Gray's interview. Not much about The Process was known. But Gray's basic argument about it was true. It stopped aging and pain, but it did not stop death.

For a second, Syl envisioned a world without pain. A world where nobody could tell when a person was dying, not even that person himself. So—what? she thought. A woman buys orange juice in the grocery store, a man gets a haircut, a mother kisses her son, and the next instant, all those people are gone?

Syl spent the afternoon coordinating a special broadcast for the sixtieth anniversary of Marks Island. Not the land itself but the discovery of it.

Everyone in town had become fascinated with the story of Marks Island recently, though no one alive had known this land when it was an island at all. That was tens of thousands of years ago. Seismic activity changed the geography, and the city grew with all its people, and, for generations, none of them thought twice about the bit of land that jutted out into the ocean. Nobody asked why the city was shaped like a lowercase *i* with the dot never fully separated from the line but coming close at high tide.

Abe was about J. P.'s age when Francis Marks found the caves with human remains, and the truth of their history washed over them. Abe said it was a phenomenon. News crews came to the beach to report on the finding and the town itself was renamed. Syl loved this, the past being reported as news. Abe loved it too. He said the discovery was the main reason that he had become a historian.

The special broadcast would include an interview with Kevin Marks, Francis Marks's grandson. He owned the museum on Marks Island. Syl read the transcript over and over. She completely lost track of time.

"Who would you recommend visit the museum?" the interviewer asked, in the transcript.

"Everyone," Kevin Marks said. "Everyone should visit. We get caught up in the future. We end up not noticing what's slipping behind. It's nice to look at artifacts every now and then, isn't it? To spend a few moments inhabiting a place that is filled with our past?"

YEAR AFTER YEAR, THE same routine as a field trip chaperone. The same buses moving slowly through downtown Marks Island City. The same sticky seats with rips in the backs and duct tape crossed over them. The same windows that opened like jawbones and hurt the pads of fingers to unlock.

Syl sat beside J. P., who was not too old yet to sit with his mother instead of his friends. Evangeline, their neighbor, sat alone in the seat across the aisle.

"What do birds do when it rains?" J. P. asked. Syl had no idea why he was asking. There were no birds in the parking lot. There were no signs of rain.

It was thirty-five minutes to Marks Island. They played bus games. The children sang call-and-response songs, filling the bus with a synchronized shouting. The rituals of fourth graders. They clapped hands on laps to keep the rhythm. When they merged onto the causeway, they sang a song about Marks Island.

A memory: Syl singing this same song in grade school on a school trip to the island—before there was even a museum on that land to visit.

"Have you been to Marks?" ("Yes, ma'am.")

"How did you get to Marks?" ("I swam.")

"When was your journey?" ("Back twelve years.")

"What was it like there?" ("Not like here.")

"That's how you get to Marks."

In each verse, the same questions were met with new responses. The journey became more and more recent. They got there by boat, by bridge, by road, and, finally, they just walked right over. The island grew increasingly familiar with each repetition. It was a strange land, an odd spot, a quaint place until, in the last verse, what was it like there? Just like here.

Evangeline did not know this song and was visibly annoyed by it. She sighed loudly and rolled her eyes. The girl had moved in with her grandfather last summer and Syl did not know the full story behind that. She'd found Evangeline rude and impatient, and yet she liked her tremendously. She seemed strong-willed with a tough exterior that Syl hoped would be a good influence on her often-oversensitive son. She was glad their families had begun carpooling.

Now, Evangeline shook her head at Syl with a pleading expression as if to say, *Can you make them shut up back there?*

And Syl smiled and shrugged to say, *Sorry. It's out of my hands.*

If Abe were a chaperone on this field trip, he would not have known the song either. This was how their gap of time was also a kind of distance. The years between them were years apart, years that separated. Syl could feel it in the bits of history that she'd studied in school but that Abe had lived through. In the slang she peppered into conversation that he needed her to translate. In his own idioms, with their archaic violence: skinning cats, stoning birds. Where did he come from with such phrases? They clashed so harshly with his kind, pale eyes.

When Marks Island was really an island, people lived there. A single tribe that may have evolved independently.

"No, it was certainly not divergent evolution."

Here was Kevin Marks—the museum owner—correcting Syl an hour later. Editing his words for the special anniversary broadcast, she'd imagined liking this man. But from this first impression, she didn't like him at all.

Kevin spoke in a monotone that still managed to sound condescending. The museum was large and pristine, and the exhibits unchanging, and, Syl thought, Kevin must spend each day giving the same tour to groups just like theirs.

"Divergent evolution would take a much, much longer time," he said.

Okay, not diverging from other humans. Just living alone.

They spent an hour wandering through the wings, hearing the stories Kevin told, and Syl warmed to him. He cared deeply about the past he was preserving; she could see that. And he was good with Evangeline, who had been acting out.

This year, just as Abe had thought, the Caves of Adina were open. They had been damaged by last fall's tremors, so the class had to divide into small groups and take turns going in. Syl stayed aboveground. She did not need to see the caves. She had seen them before.

"You're not coming?" J. P. asked.

"No," she said. "But you'll like it down there. It's neat."

These were the caves that Francis Marks had discovered and named for his wife. They might have once been some kind of ancient tunnel, very likely man-made. Or they might have been used as burial grounds for the people of Marks Island. There were several theories, many mysteries. They'd collapsed in a massive earthquake and been hidden for years.

Francis Marks had found a dozen bodies in the caves, but none of them were children. Only one child had been found anywhere on the island, and not a real boy either: a doll.

They called the doll Xumu. He was in a sleeping posture and had been dressed to look like a prince. He had a crown and long, carved nails and was covered in beautiful red stones. Syl found him fascinating. Who was he, this little prince? And where were the real children?

The human remains were of eleven men and women in their twenties or thirties, and one much older man. Papa Marks, as he was called. His body revealed a chronic ailment. And this was the part that excited Abe most. Abe had focused his studies on the role of pain in human history and had gone on to write a book on the subject.

Papa Marks had suffered a degenerative joint condition yet lived far longer than anyone else. This was, Abe claimed, the most important finding of the excavation on Marks Island.

"Like an ancient arthritis," he had told Syl years before.

A MEMORY: ABE AND Syl visiting the caves as a younger couple. Here was Abe acting as if the remains of that man were dug up yesterday, or were still being dug up today. History was that alive to him.

"To survive at all, he needed the help of his tribe. He was in his sixties when he died." Abe found this fact incredible. It was a remarkable age for an ancient human. Did she understand that? "Like being over one hundred today."

So a sick man lived for a long time a long time ago. Why was that groundbreaking?

"Further evidence of altruism among our ancestors," Abe said, sounding like a research paper. "Do you see? For years, his tribe must have helped him. They would have had to lift him into the caves. It supports the theory that altruism is inherently human."

"I don't think it was altruistic." Syl was thinking aloud. "Not necessarily. I don't think we can say that for sure."

"We can say it," Abe said. "Trust me. We can."

He had this frustrated tone that irked her, as if she were not understanding instead of just disagreeing with him. And who was this "we" he was suddenly speaking for?

Syl didn't think she should have to explain but she tried anyway. "Abe," she said, "think about us. If you were in pain and I helped you, it wouldn't be for you and you only, would it? If I'm helping you to not suffer, isn't that also for me?"

This resonated, she could tell. But he didn't want to concede his version of humanity. It was a beautiful, compelling version. But that didn't mean it was true.

"I don't think so," he said. "I don't think it would still be for you."

A new feeling, their being at odds with each other. They did not speak for a time and when they did speak, the fight flared back up.

"All I'm saying," she tried later, "is that people have all sorts of reasons for doing anything."

"So?" Abe almost laughed, not seeing what this had to do with the subject.

"I don't think altruism is something a stranger can recognize in you. I think it's one of those things, Abe," she said, "like a memory. A thing you cannot really share with anyone else."

She saw him soften. "That's a very Syl point to make."

Abe was always noting this aspect of Syl. What he called her belief in a "true human loneliness." He'd said it was why he loved her the way that he did. He wanted to inhabit that solitude at the core of her. But if he could, then it would be lost.

That was it. Their first fight. They were both so relieved when it ended that they failed to notice that it wasn't resolved. There was no answer to the question of altruism. They could drop it, but it would not go away.

THE BUS BACK TO school was quiet. They drove toward the sun and the kids closed their eyes. Some fell asleep. They passed the billboards for Prosyntus and J. P. put his head on her shoulder. She could feel the spiral of J. P.'s ear by her collarbone. He was so young. Here were his little legs on the bus seat. His feet, flat like his father's. She pictured Abe's feet as if she were holding them. It wasn't just the shape of his feet but the level plane of skin that wrapped around them. They were always cold like slabs of marble. She loved Abe's feet, loved touching them, though she knew that their flatness caused him great pain in his knees and his back.

A memory: their first apartment, hers and Abe's. It was a dim basement with cardboard boxes stacked in small towers for lack of floor. The damp smell of it, masked by candles. Syl's hands on Abe's feet, rubbing in slow circles. She was savoring that creamy softness. It reminded her of a baby they hadn't yet had. It might have been daybreak or midafternoon. There were no windows.

Imagination was so close to memory. When you pictured the future hard enough, it could feel like the past.

SYL WAS IN HER office, reading the transcript of an interview.

The interview subject was Luke Roman, set to be the youngest man to have Prosyntus.

"Why Prosyntus?" the interviewer asked. "And why now? You could wait, you know. You're still young."

Roman did not answer directly. He said he was a newlywed and then a widower in the span of a few years. He spoke of his late wife. How brave she was throughout her illness, choosing to die on her own terms.

"You must miss her."

A stupid comment, Syl thought.

"Of course I miss her. I don't want to also miss the person I was when I was with her."

"That's the reason you'll be having it?"

"One reason."

He was young to have suffered such loss, Syl thought. She could understand why he felt pulled to freeze time around him. But he came across as also, what? Naive? Shortsighted? A bit selfish, at the very least. The dead did not grow any older while the living must.

She thought of her own mother, who had begun dying by losing her memory, losing her connection to time altogether.

One day, her mother asked a doctor, "Who is the president of the country today?" and they all had a good, sad laugh about that. She kept forgetting that her husband was dead, and this fact was newly devastating for her to learn.

Throughout it all, her mother's body was still healthy, strong. She might have lived for decades if not for her mind. Eventually, forgetting became a kind of cave that she lived inside. It kept her out of the blinding brightness of today. Why should she have to know for certain how the world had changed since she was a child? She knew, with certainty, that she once was a child who lived in the world. Wasn't that enough? Syl thought it should be.

A memory: her mother, looking the way she always looked—and yet, dying. Syl pretending to be her mother's mother because that was what her mother believed.

"Mom," her mother said, holding on to Syl's hand.

Mom, Syl repeated inside her head, holding on until her mother let go.

At her desk, Syl quizzed herself for a few minutes. She imagined Abe without looking at his photograph. Discrete pieces.

The square shape of his thumbnails, the smooth border of his hairline, the shallow crease around the skin of his neck. She could build him from memory this way if she wanted to. Bit by bit. But why would she want to? There would be no need to. Not anymore. Not even if, like her mother, she started forgetting. Abe would always look the same after The Process. So there would be nothing for her to long for or miss. Only all of him, later.

Had Abe looked younger when she'd first met him? She didn't think so. When they had sex for the first time, something was wrong with Abe's left knee. She remembered his joint creaking more than the bedsprings. Hearing it, they couldn't help but laugh. And the third or fourth time, when she assumed that the awkward part was behind them, and they managed to place their bodies together and even laughed while doing so. When she rolled onto his left leg, just slightly, and his pale eyes filled up with pain. There it was: that distance. Syl had said sorry, pulled away from him. Abe had swallowed, breathed hard, swallowed again. Their bodies parallel, not touching for a moment. The feeling of vertigo as she looked down from the bed. These fragments that cohered to become a memory.

"Abe," she had said last night before falling asleep, "how will we know how much time we have left together?"

"We won't," he told her. His voice was like water. "But you know, we never could."

After her mother's death, Syl had begun collecting mementos. The plastic souvenirs from their honeymoon, for instance; she dug them up and put them on a shelf and reminded Abe how they'd come to possess them, those three figurines with their bobbling heads. For some reason, Syl thought of this now. How she took the photo album from their wedding—a book of posed smiles and blurs of movement—and wrote down every guest's name. How she made a dozen home movies documenting J. P. as a baby: J. P. saying nonsense; J. P. eating mushed fruit; J. P. doing nothing remarkable, just lying on his back in his crib blowing bubbles of spit. They had never watched these home movies. But the point was never to watch them. The point had been to make them exist.

IT WAS ABE'S TURN to make dinner and Syl sat, just watching.

"What's going on?" J. P. asked as he entered the too-quiet kitchen.

"Nothing," Syl said. Though clearly, there was something. Abe dropped a knife and it clanged against the floor.

"J. P.," Abe said, serving each of them salad from a wooden bowl, "tell me about the field trip."

J. P. lit up and started talking. He was caught on one detail—a display of the geologic timeline at the museum. Abe ate, grabbing a dinner roll in each bearlike paw, and the meal became a typical family dinner, like thousands of others. Syl thought she would confuse and forget the details of this one particular night.

She hadn't even noticed the geologic timeline that J. P. was describing. She'd been too busy learning the mechanism of human evolution. Relearning it, since, surely, she had known it all once. And what was the evolutionary advantage of forgetting? There must have been one, but she could not imagine just now what it could be.

The geologic timeline measured the history of the planet by the layers of fossils found in the rock. These, J. P. said, could be read like a story. Abe found a pen from a junk drawer and gave J. P. a fresh napkin.

"Draw it for us," he said.

J. P. drew a circle, which was surprising. Syl had been expecting a line. He divided the perimeter of the circle in two.

"These are eons," J. P. told them, "the largest units of time."

He drew arcs that went around the circle on the outside, concentric. Shorter than the hemispheres below. "Next are eras."

Another series of arcs, above the last, shorter still, with almost no curve. "Then periods." Another, still shorter. "Epochs."

And finally, no more arcs, just one vertical line. It touched the surface of the original circle at a single point. "And this is an age, the smallest unit of time."

Typical Abe. He knew all this and was eager to capture his son's interest and open it wider. He took the napkin and placed it next to the salad bowl as a centerpiece. "Look," he said and began to lecture.

He spoke of Marks Island. Of the span of time when it existed as an island. It was immeasurably small. How, if the distance from his nose to the tip of his hand were the life of this planet, then a stroke on a nail file would erase human history entirely. And wasn't that something?

Abe didn't appear to notice J. P. hunching over his plate. He didn't stop to ask if J. P. was okay. J. P. was not okay. He hated when his father did this. They both did. Syl waited for J. P. to yell out or cry. But he didn't. He pressed his lips together and stared at his lap.

"The thing about this timeline," Abe concluded at long last, "is that it's relative. Every span of time is bound by a major event—a mass extinction, for instance, the age of the dinosaur. It is not absolute. They call it 'deep time,'" he said. "Did you know that, J.? Like deep space or the deep sea?"

"Mmm," J. P. said. He got up to clear the table.

"Thanks," Abe called, catching Syl's eye.

"You can leave it in the sink," Syl told him. "Finish your homework, please."

Only the two of them in the kitchen. Abe's hair almost glowed, it was so white. Syl didn't know when exactly it had become that color, but it had happened.

She felt angry with Abe for making J. P. feel so little so quick, but Abe preempted her. "I know," he said. He looked bewildered. "I'm sorry. I got carried away."

They'd never built a good method for fighting. There'd been that one lasting argument about the ancient old man. Before that, eons ago, there was the mild bickering over the boundaries of their shared existence. Someone's dirty socks falling short of the hamper, someone's used tissues on the bathroom sink. It was almost nice, those bodily signs of their life together.

So Abe was sorry. Good, but why was he telling her? He should tell J. P.

"I know," Abe said again. "I need to tell him."

After he left the kitchen, Syl wondered what Abe was telling their son. That he was sorry for the lecture or that he was having The Process, or both? That the appointment was just hours away now?

J. P.'s drawing was still on the table. There was the wobbly nature of J. P.'s writing. The arcs around the circle looked like a pulse. A shred of lettuce had fallen onto it. Syl peeled it off.

An age.

It was all the time they were going to have, she and Abe. Just a slice of one. And this was it, right now. They were living through it. The Age of Sylvia and Abraham. What major event would mark their ending? And when? There had never been any way to predict.

HERE IT WAS: THE day Abe began The Process. On the cabinet, a sticky note with two words, "Don't forget." And she wouldn't. She hunted for details to remember so she could trace it all back later to now.

"Wake up, Syl." That was Abe's voice. "Wake up," he said. "It's a beautiful day." He'd been saying this forever, since they lived in the basement with no view of the sky. He'd say it, facing their square of white ceiling, and Syl would laugh and ask, "How can you tell?"

One of Abe's feet grazed her bare legs below the covers. Flat, smooth. A flash of nightmare—touched by something she did not recognize, something lifeless and yet not dead.

What else? The sweater he was wearing at breakfast. The swirling pattern on it. The gallon of milk on the counter. It was past its expiration but it smelled like nothing at all.

"Abe," Syl said to his back as he rinsed the dishes. He did not hear her but she was asking if he felt scared.

And in the future, what would she remember? After that gallon of milk was depleted, another one filling its place on the door of the fridge? Later still. How would imagination distort this memory?

This evening she would meet J. P. after practice. She would stand outside the gymnasium waiting for him. The sound of happy yells would echo inside her chest. And she would remember that.

There was the drive to work. The view from the office. The ache in her wrists while she was typing. The mundaneness of her job, which could be any job, on this day, which could be any day. But it was not any day. Because she was here while Abe was taking a city bus to the facility, and this was the moment when things began changing. The moment when things stopped changing at all.

There was still work to be done and she was still doing it. A review of Monique Gray's newest artwork, an interview with a seismologist who theorized that Marks Island was overdue for an earthquake. Tomorrow would be the anniversary broadcast too. Sixty years of ancient Marks Island. Updated copies flew to her desk.

There would be a segment on the tribe that lived on the island. Syl had many questions that the piece did not answer. How had it felt for the tribe to live with that old man, Papa Marks, among them? To help him for so many years. Was it a burden? Probably. But not enough of one to stop helping him, certainly not. And if they could have changed it, would they? Or did they accept it without thinking that their lives could be anything else? Suddenly, it was dark and Syl needed to pick up J. P.

The drive was a blurred strip of asphalt that Syl did not remember because here she was already at school. The gym door swung shut heavily.

"Hi, Mom."

J. P. was wearing a knee brace.

"What happened?" Syl asked.

"Nothing happened," he said. "It just hurts."

As they neared home, things slowed down again.

There were J. P.'s eyes in the rearview. Pale blue, just like Abe's. She wished that they looked more like her own—deep, dark pits in shades of brown soil. She sighed and began telling him what his father had done, was doing. Healthy boyhood sweat filled the car. That smell, she thought, would define this moment for both of them in retrospect.

J. P. interrupted. "He told me, Mom. I already know. It's okay." The scene she had imagined inverted: J. P. was comforting her.

"But, Mom," J. P. said, when she pulled into their driveway and waited for him to go inside. "I want to come with you."

The drive to the facility would be the end of a chapter. Syl had imagined she'd be alone first, then with Abe, and then the three of them would be all together again. It was the right order for the next chapter to start.

J. P. sat on his fingertips, seat belt still on. His voice cracked when he said, "Please."

"No, J." Syl knew this was selfish. "Trust me. You should wait at home. We'll be back in an hour."

J. P. unbuckled and walked to the front door. He turned back, looked at Syl, and waved.

The facility was a monolith of glass and steel across from the sea. The waiting room was uncomfortably bright. On TV, a teaser for the anniversary broadcast. A historical re-creation of Papa Marks, what he might have looked like, and a photo of the little boy doll.

Syl thought of the tribe, how they carried the old man into the caves. Did it make him feel helpless? Syl wondered.

It was a remarkably old age, the host was saying.

Yes, Syl knew, like one hundred today.

But did he have a wife? Was she younger than he was? Children? No, there were no children on ancient Marks Island, she knew that. But maybe there was one child they had dreamed of but who had never come? And the wife, had she pictured the future of her husband's ailment? Was that a fundamental piece of the person she was? Even so, picturing it wouldn't have shaped how it happened. She must have discovered that. That you could never imagine your way to a future memory.

Abe appeared and stood beside her. She got up and they kissed.

"That was the first kiss of the rest of our lives," Syl said. She meant this to be funny, but it came out flat.

"How do you feel?" She cleared her throat.

"Great," he said.

Syl said, "Good." She kissed him to replace the first one that had turned stale already.

J. P. did not come running to the door when he heard the car park. They found him sitting in the living room with the TV volume turned down.

"J.," Abe said.

J. P.'s eyebrows lifted. "Dad," he said. "You're okay?"

Abe sat beside his son. "I'm just fine."

J. P. stared at Abe and Abe stared at J. P. and they hugged. Syl found the remote and turned the volume up. It was the ending of a movie they'd all seen before. J. P. and Abe were talking, low and fast, laughing together, relieved. But Syl didn't listen. She'd forgotten the premise of the film. Who were these characters? How were they related? Why were they doing the things that they did?

J. P. ate leftover fries from a Styrofoam container, sitting on the floor with his back against the couch. Abe reached over to grab a handful but dropped them because they were cold.

"Ew," Abe complained. "How can you eat them like that?"

J. P. faced forward. "Like what?" He ate four at once. "They taste good." There was ketchup on J. P.'s lips that looked like blood.

"J. P.," Abe said, "wipe your face."

J. P. stuck his tongue out and licked it.

"J. P., please," Syl said. It might have been the first thing she'd said since they came home.

The late-night news was on and she and Abe watched it after J. P. went to bed.

Sources were saying Monique Gray would be having The Process soon. The anchor did not know what to make of this development. Was it performance art?

A clip from her recent appearance on *Time Line* replayed.

"It's a curse," she was saying.

Luke Roman had had his first injection, they reported next. He was the youngest person to have the procedure and he was having a strange symptom since returning home: he had lost parts of his long-term memory. A doctor from the facility appeared on the program as a guest expert. He said, reassuringly, that this would be a temporary reaction. Nothing serious.

"It's scary," Roman said. "I don't remember my life."

Or did he say "wife"?

A commercial break. A supermodel spoke of her life since The Process. How her extensive skin-care regimen was obsolete. All she needed now was sunscreen.

"So," Syl said, searching for something else they might talk about. Anything else.

"So," Abe said. "So it's not that different, right? And it'll never be different again."

SOME MEMORIES: TWENTY-THREE YEARS. It was always there. And yet. The day Abe had The Process. All the details she would forget and write over. The palimpsest of memory. How they returned to the Caves of Adina. How they fought without fighting, without even approaching their situation, their selves.

"That ancient man," Syl was saying, "Papa Marks, his pain is what kept him alive. Because his tribe knew about it. They helped him. And then he lived."

"And his tribe?" Abe was asking. "What good did his suffering do for his tribe?"

He spoke as though he were the expert on this. Syl wanted to scream at him. You could not make an academic study of someone else's pain.

The pattern on his sweater. How it made her dizzy. The vertigo of looking down from the bed when she'd hurt his knee. How his body would no longer anchor her to any one clear time or place. And was it selfish to want that? What would happen if she began forgetting the way her mother had?

"Death," Abe was saying. "It's one of those things, Syl. Things that cannot be shared." How he sounded almost happy, like he finally understood something.

And how this conversation brought Syl back to their baby. To J. P. when he was brand new, a minute old, when he did not yet have a name. And backward from that point, to being in labor, to the pain like a solid wall that, without warning, would crumble around her and be forgotten as soon as it was gone. While for J. P., it had all been simple. Like crossing a threshold.

"Why not make it easier?" Abe was saying.

Easier for whom? That should have been her next question. But she thought she knew and did not have to ask.

Here was Syl, the pigment gone from her hair and her brown eyes fogged so they looked more like dust than soil. Life continued and nothing changed very much except for once, when the gap was closed, finally.

Twenty-three years felt like forever. She waited for the day when there would be no time between her and Abe. But the moment came and the days kept passing and she kept growing older. Why?

Because Abe was gone already. She found this fact especially hard to remember.

And because Prosyntus was a spectacular failure. There were side effects nobody expected. Rare but permanent memory loss in the younger patients especially. Luke Roman never did recover his memory. And for older patients, there was sudden death with no clear cause. For Abe, it happened in an instant without any warning. He was in their foyer, unzipping his raincoat.

The procedure was pulled from the market. There was a class-action lawsuit. A settlement that didn't bring anyone or their memories back.

More and more time passed. Syl grew old, older than Abe. That is, her body grew older than his ever would. Did she know this? Sometimes she did. But mostly, she was lost in a deep time where there was no Process. She was in their first apartment. She was rubbing her wrinkled hands on someone else's skin.

J. P. was a man and not even a young one. He grew tall and thin like his father, the same bad knees, the same flat feet. He moved far away and she saw him once or twice yearly. When Syl looked at her son, she saw the man she fell in love with. When she looked for the man she fell in love with, she could not find him. Where was the person she was supposed to grow old with?

And now, here she is, holding a very small child. He is red, small, asleep, covered in stone.

"It's going to be a beautiful day," someone is saying. Who is saying that? Where are they?

She is in a wide room that feels familiar. There are no windows. There's a musty smell of fresh soil, of caves.

"Wake up," says a voice. And she should, she knows. She should wake up. She is trying to.

And here—another child, even younger somehow, sleeping inside the caves.

PART TWO

–9–

Thirty years before Maeve's sleep

KEVIN'S BIGGEST REGRET IN LIFE WAS THAT HE WAS not born a Francis. He didn't seem to have what a Francis must have, which he grew up believing was the power to leave an impression on history. He was not like Francis Crick or Bacon or Drake or Scott Key. And he was not like Francis Marks Sr., his grandfather, or Francis Marks Jr., his father, either.

Francis Jr. had named him Kevin, but was "Kevin" a name strong enough to hold any significant weight? He feared it was not.

At age nine, with this question first gnawing at him, Kevin slunk to the garden to find his grandmother.

"How many famous Kevins are there, Gran?" he asked.

Before she could answer, he clarified, "And don't say that actor from those movies we only see ads for."

Adina wiped her forehead and stood from her squat. "Which Kevins can I say then, Kevin?" she asked.

"Ones from history."

Adina exhaled and reminded Kevin that she was never any good at remembering names and she was no student of history either.

So he would inherit nothing from the Francises that came before him. Was that it? Francis Marks Jr., who had studied ancient organisms all over the world, and Francis Marks Sr., who had focused his attention more locally and made his big discovery right here in a city that was now named for him.

To hear Adina tell of Francis Sr.'s great discovery was to gain a more intimate view than any historian could provide. It was the one family story Adina had shared, and Kevin made her tell it often though he knew it by heart.

When Francis Sr. was not yet Francis Sr. but only Francis, he abandoned Adina, then pregnant, to go to the end of a strip of land and dig a deep ditch.

"What if you're wrong?" Adina asked, full of bitterness. "What if what you're looking for isn't there?"

She was afraid that her stubborn husband might keep digging forever under the conviction that he was correct.

"I'm not wrong," he told her, not helping dispel her worry as he grabbed whichever shovel was nearest before tying his boots.

"If you die out there, I am not going to bury you," Adina said. "You can lie right down in that hole you're digging. I won't even come to cover your body with dirt." She whispered her anger so the neighbors wouldn't hear it.

The end of Adina's story was Kevin's favorite part.

On the night of the discovery, Adina baked Francis's favorite meal, a potpie, and they had a quiet celebration at home. His hands were so thick and callused from months of digging that he could feel nothing from them, not pain and not pressure. When the timer rang out, he took the dish straight from the oven with his bare hands, forgoing a mitt.

By thirteen, Kevin had mostly reconciled himself to the fact that he wasn't a Francis. It was okay for his own sake, but what of his father and grandfather's legacy? It was largely for them that he went into museum work. His grandfather's shovel, his boots, and that baking dish—those were his first acquisitions.

He envisioned the museum he'd build as a castle filled with treasures of these great men that everyone would be eager to see.

Was Kevin happy?

He still believed he could be when he went off to pursue his studies: preservation, conservation, and curation. He immersed himself in the science of his chosen field. It was not paleoanthropology (his grandfather's science), and it was not evolutionary biology (his father's science), nor was it any of the newly emerging sciences of the day—alchemical engineering or nanocryogenics. Nonetheless, Kevin learned which substances to apply to keep bone intact, which to use to stop flesh from rotting, and relevant questions from disciplines like philosophical phenomenology (how do museum visitors articulate their experience through an inarticulate body?) and, more practically, textiles (how many days are lost from the life of a medieval tapestry when it is exposed to a single hour of natural light?).

He returned home when Adina died. After that, he drew up plans for the museum and rapidly expanded his collection of artifacts.

He had the Marks Museum of Human History built around the hollowed-out structures where the ancient humans were found. Francis Sr. had named these the Caves of Adina, though his grandmother had hated them.

"The past is gone," she would say. "Why try to claim it?"

Kevin had these caves reinforced so that his visitors could enter them on guided tours of the museum's collections. He hired two part-time employees to clean the bathrooms and manage the cafeteria for ten hours each week.

They did their jobs, but he never saw them. Artifacts from the two great men he never knew took up most of the building's four wings, and with that pit at the center and barely any visitors save field trips of students, it was more like a mausoleum than a museum.

In those early years, Kevin took a quiet pride in his work. He hung portraits of the Francises on the wall of his office, and the disappointment of being born a Kevin was temporarily quelled; he wasn't a Francis, no, but he was a Marks after all. The past was not gone, he thought. Adina was wrong about that. Because here he was, reclaiming it and preserving it.

There was a specific nostalgia to the work that he took pleasure in too. Being inside his museum brought him back to his boyhood spent in his grandmother's kitchen. To the refrigerator, which she'd kept pristine, everything in its proper place, the crisper with its vibrant orbs of yellow and red and all shades of green. When the door was open, it was an immaculate display, spotlit and arranged to be viewed. Kevin had longed to glimpse into that refrigerator when it was closed.

What did it all look like when no one was looking? He would put his head against the doorjamb and squint with one eye. Were the juice and milk still lined up on the top shelf, and all of the dozen eggs (somehow, always a full dozen) nested safely in the egg bins, and whichever berry variety was ripe and ready for dessert that night, were they wet and glistening even and especially when no one was looking at them with their two hungry eyes?

In those first years at the museum, he felt like he had finally done this: slipped inside a closed fridge. He was there, in the dark world of objects. He could hold his breath in this suspended animation, feeling as though he were another object, some simple artifact from someone else's past, and that now he must wait patiently for the door to open and the lights to turn on and a visitor to find her way in.

Kevin had studied many fields of art and science to become a museum owner, but he had not studied business. He'd put most of his inheritance into the construction and expansion of his collections. But the museum was proving financially unsustainable. By the third year, when the field trips thinned in the winter and the museum had no visitors at all for three weeks, he had to fire his two employees.

He sank into a deep sadness. He thought of the way he'd envisioned this life. The museum as a castle. Throngs of people eager to see the treasures it held. And how widely he was failing at this. He was going to have to shutter the place soon, and then what would happen to the history he thought he was meant to be keeping?

He was in his office, confronting the awful state of the finances, when he got the call.

The Siegler family wanted to make a donation. Siegler—Kevin knew the name. They were wealthy philanthropists and political donors. The opera house downtown was named for them; also an art gallery near the city university. They had made their fortune in pharmaceuticals and biotech and owned several companies.

The executive on the phone explained the family's preferred donor relationship.

The Sieglers would give him an anonymous monthly sum, and in exchange, they wanted access to Grace Beach, the private land behind the museum.

What would they do with the land?

That was the one question Kevin asked on that phone call.

"They won't build anything," said the man. "But you can't ask any other questions." He spoke in a low tone. "And you can't go there. That would all be part of this deal."

Kevin was quiet and the man on the phone repeated the sum. "Monthly," he added, unnecessarily.

It would be enough to keep the museum from closing. Maybe even to make some renovations down the line. There were no windows facing Grace Beach anyway; visitors would never see whatever it was the Sieglers would do there, and neither would he.

"What do you say?" the man asked.

And Kevin said yes.

Nothing changed dramatically after that phone call. Not right away. Kevin no longer felt paralyzed when sitting down to do the accounting. The Siegler donations took the pressure off, but his museum was still mostly empty.

When the sea and wind were calm toward the evening, he could hear a noise that sounded like drilling, but he stayed off that stretch of the beach, as he had agreed. On his morning walks, he found strange rocks washing up south of Grace Beach. They didn't look like any other rocks on the local beaches, but they were not unfamiliar to him; there were rocks just like it inside his museum as part of an ancient artifact, a sleeping doll that looked like a prince. The rocks were glittery and blood red and made him think of a meteorite. There was something almost otherworldly about them.

One morning, he found a small one that was especially bright and crimson. For no real reason, he picked it up and put it in his pocket.

He carried it around with him. On the slowest days, he turned the rock over in his hands and wondered what the Sieglers were doing to make chunks of earth like this appear, but then he'd tell himself it was best to hold on to some questions without trying to answer them. He'd place the rock in his pocket again.

A few years into this arrangement, things did change more dramatically: museums became popular. New donations and new patrons streamed in. Field trips had to schedule early so he would not overbook. Couples started calling, wanting to know the costs associated with hosting their weddings in the museum.

He was a bit bewildered by this, though he knew that it was part of a broader trend that had been going on for some time.

Old things were back in style. There were retro diners opening downtown. A woolly mammoth was set to be reanimated. Kevin had seen teenagers wearing the same kind of hat Adina used to wear—those boxy things that perched precariously on the top of their heads.

And behind all this, there was one of the Sieglers' companies, Genesix. They were rumored to be developing a new procedure that would stop a person from growing physically older and block chronic pain. It was all anyone was talking about. Preservation was, apparently, hip.

They would soon be approaching a milestone anniversary of Francis Sr.'s discovery too, and the city was making a multiyear event out of this. They'd hung banners on the streetlights downtown and taken out ads to promote free concerts, carnivals, and fireworks that would lead up to what they were calling Founders Day.

Kevin took advantage of the trend too. He commissioned an artist to make a pencil drawing of his grandfather's face and he had this printed on posters and novelty mugs, which he sold in his gift shop.

Visitors often engaged him in long conversations as they shopped. Once, a young woman came in with her husband and spoke to him for nearly two hours. She looked sickly, but her eyes were animated as she listened to him speak of the past. She had a book of lists that she showed him. He loved reading through these lists, which were like her personal historical records.

One afternoon, the mayor's office called to ask if they could host their Founders Day gala inside his museum.

"We'll pay, of course," they said. Genesix would be the main sponsor.

"Sure," Kevin said. "Let me just make sure there's not a wedding that day." He laughed, hearing himself booking events so far in advance.

But when he hung up, he had an uneasy thought: First the monthly donation, then the Genesix procedure making museums popular, and now this gala bringing all kinds of publicity—why were the Sieglers behind all his success?

It was that same week, a day or two later, that he saw the newspaper headline.

He tore the article out and folded it and put it in his chest pocket. He distracted himself with the bus of first graders who'd just arrived for the morning's field trip.

Usually such young children quickly exhausted his patience, but that day, he let their squeaky, shuffling sneakers push away what he no longer wished to think about. All afternoon, he welcomed their interruptions.

"Ooh, ooh!" they called out, hands waving wildly.

"Yes?" he would say, selecting a child.

"Um," and then the instant deflation, the arm retracting. "Um," they'd say, "um . . . I forget."

But a field trip of first graders cannot last forever. It can hardly last three hours.

"What do we say to Mr. Marks?" their teacher prompted, as they lined up two by two in the lobby.

"Thank you, Mr. Marks," they chanted, low and asynchronous, as they marched out.

Back at his desk by the light of his banker's lamp, he took out the article.

Dr. Naomi Wilhelm, Researcher at Genesix, Dead in Apparent Suicide

Kevin read quickly, hungry for details. The woman had drowned. A fisherman had found her body. She'd had rocks in her pockets and the presumption was that it was suicide. She'd written no note. She left behind a family. She had been working at Genesix for several years.

He reread the piece twice. The rocks in this woman's pockets, the article made a point of describing them. They were a unique type that did not seem to be native to the region: crimson with a metallic luster.

There was a mystery in this woman's death and Kevin had no interest in solving it, but he could not stop his mind from whirling toward it.

She'd worked at Genesix. And those rocks. Why *those* rocks? Could she have been coming from Grace Beach? It was right across the narrow bay from where her body was found.

He took the rock from his own pocket and stared at it, as if willing it to speak to him. It was so red it seemed like it should be hot to the touch, like it belonged to the molten core of the planet.

He turned the article over with a swift motion. Forget it, he told himself.

There on the back was a photograph: an aerial shot of a blue whale swimming under a fishing boat. The shadow creature dwarfed the vessel, which floated, unknowing, above. The article that accompanied the image was just a list of "fun facts" about whales. It was a fluff piece. Kevin thought it would put him at ease to read it.

"A blue whale," Kevin read, "has a heart so big that a person could swim through its valves."

It was difficult to imagine that—a heart so big. He paused for a minute.

He imagined the vastness of the ocean, the enormity of the whale, and the humans aboard that speck of a boat. He felt a bit seasick. From aboard that vessel, he thought, the whale would have looked like a dark patch of ocean and not the largest living animal that exists.

The brevity of human history felt very real to him all of a sudden. As soon as a person exists, they start disappearing, he thought. And a heart, even a huge blue whale heart, it is, in essence, a timer and every beat only counts down.

We are so small, he thought, on the scale of almost anything. And in the end, there is always an end. Was that right?

He heard the drilling outside and he pictured the drills unearthing his oldest fear about his own tiny existence and all his life's work, the failure of being a Kevin.

That woman who'd drowned, Dr. Wilhelm. And those rocks. Why *those* rocks? he thought again and again. He hung the article in his office so that he could reread it, if he wanted to. But he never wanted to, and he faced the page so it was the blue whale he saw.

In the months that followed, as he sat at his desk and processed the paperwork and deposited the monthly checks from the Sieglers, which he was still allowing to flow in, he'd look up at his father and grandfather in the portraits hanging beside the blue whale. The three of them reminded him of his own smallness. He kept the rock in his pocket.

He slept in his museum on most nights. It was the only place he found he could let his mind rest. He would wander around, passing all the exhibits and artifacts that he'd been telling the same stories about day after day.

He would go to the archives in the basement and sit in rooms that were climate- and light-controlled and that he was not meant to sit in for more than a quarter hour for lack of real air.

Eventually, he would go down to the Caves of Adina. He pictured his grandmother's kitchen and her refrigerator. Her refusal to try to solve the mysteries of the past.

The earth was cool through his thin shirt. He kept his eyes open and stared up through the skylight at the blue stain streaked with grays and whites overhead. He tried to clear his mind of all thought, all energy. Time washed over everything as the color darkened from blue to midnight blue to dark bluish black to blackish gray and a black so black it looked almost like sleep.

-10-

Three days into Maeve's sleep

Father to Care for Girl, 8, in Mysterious Coma After Near Drowning

MARKS ISLAND BULLETIN | METRO

Eight-year-old Maeve Wilhelm has returned home though she remains in a strange comatose state. Doctors say there is no chance of recovery. They cannot explain how she is still breathing unassisted. She shows no other signs of brain function.

"I would say that yes, it's impossible for Maeve to recover. There is zero chance," said one official familiar with the team who treated Maeve at Seven Oaks Hospital. "She is still breathing, as reported. We cannot explain that."

Tragedy struck young Maeve last Sunday at the swimming pool for residents of the Jacob's Circle community. Maeve was with her family and a group of neighborhood children. Nobody saw Maeve sink to the bottom of the deep end. Once her absence was noted, around 3:30 p.m., the lifeguard on duty acted swiftly and pulled Maeve to the surface. By then, her stomach was distended and her face had turned blue.

According to an anonymous neighbor, Maeve's sister was inconsolable. "She was screaming that the bloom had killed her sister. She was talking about the algae bloom at our community beach. She might have thought that if not for that algae, they would've been at the beach instead of the pool. I don't know. It's a kid's logic."

This is not the first tragedy to befall the family in recent years. Dr. Naomi Wilhelm, Maeve's mother, died last summer in an apparent suicide by drowning at Rocky Beach Harbor.

Asked for a statement about the accident, Lionel Wilhelm, Maeve's father, declined to comment.

Maeve's body will need around-the-clock care. A special hospital bed was brought to the Wilhelms' residence yesterday. A neighbor who came out to watch the delivery said she was surprised that Mr. Wilhelm had opted to care for Maeve by himself.

"There are several high-quality care facilities much better equipped for her," the neighbor said. "I told him this. I wanted to make sure he understood his other options. I said, 'So where will you put her?' He misunderstood. He looked at me and said, 'Here. Right here in my arms.'"

WHAT DO YOU KNOW? What do you know? They began sharing what little they'd learned in the minutes and hours after the accident.

They knew that the girl had been wearing a blue bathing suit with a pattern of fish all over the front. Not the back. The back was just solid blue.

They knew that her twin had a matching suit. They had seen her in it earlier that summer. But she was not wearing hers. Not that day. Her suit had stars.

They knew that a near drowning was not a drowning. And they knew that this was not something you said after one happened, or nearly happened. They knew they should not say how things could be worse when things were already bad.

Awful.

There were some details they knew but did not contribute to this pooling of knowledge.

How by the time they pulled her out, there was vomit down the front of her face. How her hair had tinged green from the chlorine, for she'd been swimming all summer. How she'd looked like a mermaid, a monster, a corpse. How they had found her facedown, the solid color of her bathing suit blending in with the blue of the water.

Where were the parents?

They asked this to better convince themselves that bad things happened to bad people. Forget that the girl could not have been a very bad person. She was only eight. But the parents, they demanded, where were they?

The father, they said, they had never trusted him. A bug scientist and an oddball.

And the mother, wasn't she a doctor of some kind?

Not that kind of doctor, they corrected.

It doesn't matter, someone remembered, the mother is dead.

Oh. Right, yes.

How could they have forgotten the last worst thing to have happened to this same neighborhood? This same family? Now they remembered.

A horror, they said, to stop speaking ill of the family.

They would have thought a mother's suicide would be enough sadness for one family for a while. They would never have imagined there could be something new for what was left of the family to grieve and so soon.

But so—where was she now? The drowned girl.

At the hospital.

Her condition?

Extremely critical.

There was no hope. She was underwater too long. It was over, or ending.

They stood around, nodding sadly.

Any minute, they'd be pulling the plug.

EVANGELINE WOKE SURROUNDED BY flowers. Her back hurt. She reached out to touch the flowers—what were they?—but they were too far away. Her lower back throbbed like a heartbeat.

She blinked twice and saw the living room. Sunlight poured through the window, making familiar shapes on the carpet. She felt pleased to find herself there, among flowers, in those diamonds of light. And what a funny name: "living room." A room for living. Wasn't every room a living room? She wanted to say this to her sister. A joke she had made up. They were always trying to make up their own jokes. She blinked again and retrieved her focus and depth perception. The room shifted into three dimensions around her and for a moment, she saw herself as if she were dreaming. She hovered above what she did not yet remember as if standing on the surface of a foot of fresh snow.

This weightlessness lasted a second before the heart in her lower back fluttered and her vision cramped and released like a muscle: the flowers were not flowers. They were the pattern in the upholstery. She had merely fallen asleep on the living room couch.

She remembered the babysitter. It had been a long time since Evangeline had gone to sleep with a stranger in the house, and this particular babysitter was weird and nervous. She had barely spoken to the sitter the entire night. There'd been nothing to say. She remembered being surprised that the babysitter hadn't tried harder—to get her to talk or to make her sleep in her own bedroom or to do any of the things her father would have wanted a babysitter to try to do. Make Evangeline brush her teeth. Anything. What were they paying her for?

The sitter was older than seventeen. She'd admitted to this but she hadn't told the girls how old she was exactly. She smelled like boiled vegetables and she tended to wear the same thin sweater no matter the weather and she stretched it over one side of her torso and balled the sleeves into fists while crossing her arms. She would stretch the sweater out that way. Didn't she know that?

Just now, Evangeline could not remember the sitter's name. This was troubling. She couldn't ask her. Not after the sitter had spent the night in her home. She'd been watching them for a few years at this point. They knew one another and Evangeline should know, at least, her name.

She could picture her perfectly. Skinny and slightly hunched with clear skin—for a babysitter. She had a dark mole near the corner of her lip. A witch's mole. It even had a hair in it. The more she and Maeve had talked about the mole, the more they realized the sitter looked like the kind of evil witch that babysitters were hired to keep kids from thinking about before bedtime.

The girls liked to do impressions of her after she'd put them to bed, when she thought they were asleep. Evangeline was good at imitating her mannerisms while Maeve was better at mimicking her speech: a weird accent with lots of *v*'s in it, and a voice like she needed to clear her throat all the time. She gave a breathy laugh before basically every syllable. She had an annoying laugh, they agreed. The girls would take turns with these imitations for almost an hour, entertaining themselves and each other. Once, they had made the mistake of showing the sitter herself the act. They'd just wanted an audience.

Evangeline had used a marker to draw moles on each of them. "Ours don't have the hair though," she said.

"What hair?" asked the babysitter.

And Maeve said, "Never mind!"

They did their little performance for a few minutes before Evangeline realized that the babysitter was not laughing. "Wait," she said. "You don't think it's funny?"

"I do not think it's funny, no," the sitter said.

Evangeline turned to Maeve. She wasn't sure if they should apologize or feel embarrassed or what. Maeve's expression mirrored her own. They stood there, not saying anything, their comedy routine abruptly over. The sitter hadn't sounded mad or sad. Only—what? Bored?

Her back throbbed again. She could not remember hurting her back and she did not want to remember it. She got up to find the babysitter.

The babysitter was not in the armchair. Maybe she'd slept in the girls' bedroom? Maybe they'd switched places for the night? She had heard her mother complain once, over a year ago, that the babysitter often fell asleep on the living room couch.

"We don't pay the girl to sleep," her mother said.

Evangeline remembered thinking how weird it would be if they did.

Once, while playing in the yard, the babysitter had tripped and said something that sounded like a swear under her breath. Evangeline wanted to get her in trouble for swearing.

"What did you say?" she asked.

She told them that it was a word in another language, that it meant "paper cut."

The house was eerily quiet. She wasn't home alone, was she? Evangeline had never been home alone. She'd been home alone with Maeve for maybe five minutes one time. Their father had gone to the neighbors to return a casserole dish—this was after their mother died, when all the neighbors kept bringing over casseroles—and that whole five minutes, Maeve and Evangeline jumped on the beds and chanted, "Home alone! Home alone!" until the front door opened and their father returned.

"Darn it," Evangeline whined, "we wasted it."

Being home alone no longer excited her, if that was what was happening. She'd have preferred not to be alone right now. She walked down the hallway, tiptoeing so as not to startle anyone. Where was the babysitter? Outside their bedroom, she paused. She had that feeling again. That she was seeing herself in a dream. Like, if she turned the light on, there would be the two beds and the two girls and one of those girls would be her. It didn't matter which one.

She turned the light on. The beds were there, but no girls. No babysitter either. Empty. She turned the light off and kept moving through her house as if it were haunted, or no—as if *she* were the one haunting it.

The babysitter was not in the den and not in the basement and not in her father's room and not anywhere. The babysitter was nowhere. The phrase "it's always in the last place you look" came to mind. It was something their father said.

She didn't think it was true. In fact, she knew it was not true. Sometimes you looked one last place and then you stopped looking. Sometimes you didn't find what was missing, and so you gave up.

She checked the bedroom closets. She found a sweater on her father's side of the walk-in that had a white and brown pattern like cow spots. It was hideous. Last Halloween, their father had dressed up like a cow. He'd had actual udders. It was humiliating.

She looked in the closet mirror and pulled down the waistband on her pajama pants and turned so that she could see her back, which was still throbbing. Just above her butt in the center, there was a bruise, dark purplish black. Her own disgusting cow spot. She remembered now: she had run around the pool edge, screaming about her sister, and slipped. She pulled her pants up and tried to forget about the bruise and about everything else.

She checked the linen closet and the cedar closet. Each had its own particular smell—the first of fresh laundry and the second like a gerbil cage. Where did the smell come from? They did not have a gerbil.

Evangeline and Maeve had shown the babysitter the cedar closet once.

"It smells like a gerbil, right?" Maeve said.

"A gerbil?" said the babysitter. "I don't know this word."

Evangeline had turned to Maeve then like: *Is she serious?* But neither of them could explain what a gerbil was.

"It's always in the last place you look," she said because she was just getting a little scared by the emptiness and silence.

She forgot what she was looking for as she checked the cabinet under the kitchen sink. She found cleaning fluid and rubber gloves and a bottle of what looked like glue before she remembered that she should not be down there because cleaning fluid was poison, so she got up quickly and hit her head.

The babysitter was not in the bathroom, but while Evangeline was in there, she opened the medicine cabinet. She found three open boxes of bandages. One set of normal ones, one set of princess ones, and the last set with big, bold words stretched out over them. "Ouch!" these bandages said. "Whoops!" and "Uh-oh!" She took one of each of those. She put them on her face to help the pain from hitting her head even though she knew they wouldn't really help. They'd only announce to anyone—if there was anyone—that something hurt.

She walked back down the hallway, angry now. Where was that dolt of a babysitter? She retraced her steps. Under the beds in their room she found two vacuum-sealed bags of winter clothing. The bags were hard as rocks and the plastic was freezing. But inside were the softest, warmest sweaters they owned.

The bags looked like a meal a giant would be served on an airplane. This was a funny thought, but also a freaky one. She laughed to make a noise, but her laugh sounded fake.

She remembered her father putting the winter clothes in there at the turn of the season. She and Maeve were surprised that you could use a vacuum that way, to suck out air.

"What are you doing?" she had said. Or was it her sister?

Their father was holding the vacuum tube over the bag, and the bag was shrinking up like a raisin. He tried to explain over the noise of the machine that air was not empty. He told them where the word "vacuum" came from. That outer space was a vacuum. That it had sunlight and some other kinds of energy. Something something something. She couldn't hear him. The vacuum was loud. She stopped being able to understand what she did hear, so she'd just nodded. That was how you got their father to stop talking. Keep nodding, ask no questions, at some point, he'd run out of air.

She was still holding one of the bags of sweaters when she remembered the man from the ambulance the day before. She didn't want to remember him. But there had been the word "oxygen." The phrase "lack of oxygen to the brain." Her sister's brain like that bag of sweaters. All her sister's thoughts and memories getting hard and cold and the bag they were encased in wrinkling up around it, shriveling like a raisin. The sweaters were pink and gray and she didn't want to be holding them anymore.

She threw the vacuum bag onto the ground as hard as she could. It thumped down only inches away. It was heavier than it should have been, or maybe she was too weak to throw it too far.

THE WILHELMS WERE NOT her favorite family to babysit. Far from it. Maybe her least favorite. Though, to be fair, she had no favorite family to babysit. She did not like babysitting. In the movies she watched, the babysitters were peppy girls with bad hair and no friends their own age. Girls who did not make the cheer squad but kept trying year after year.

At the refugee organization, she had been told that movies were one of the best ways to master the language. On a typical day, if she was not babysitting, she might watch six movies.

She pulled her sweater around her thin body. She blamed her landlady for putting her in this predicament.

She had been walking upstairs to her one-bedroom apartment when her landlady had called from below.

"Do you babysit?"

She hadn't said no right away because she could use the money. She had very little money, almost none. But she hadn't said yes either since yes was a lie.

What she had said, at the moment, was nothing.

People in this country did not like silence. She had learned this. They would read into a silence any number of words that had never been said.

She'd said nothing and smiled and lifted her eyebrows for a single second, and then she asked her own question as if that were an answer, which was just this: "How old are the kids?"

They were never actual babies. They were usually between the ages of five and eleven. At first, she assumed this meant children did not need a babysitter by the time they turned twelve. But later, there were some twelve-year-olds also.

She herself was in her midtwenties but nobody knew it or guessed it because she looked much younger. The kids always tried to guess her age but she'd never tell them. She'd figured out from her movies that babysitters were usually teens, and so she didn't want to freak anyone out. "Freak out" was a great expression. She loved that one.

She was living alone and the assumption, again made in the gap that was her silence on the matter, was that she was a student. Studying what and at which college, nobody in the neighborhood knew or asked. Not even her landlady. It was remarkable, really, that she was trusted with their children. They knew nothing about her.

The twins were somewhere on the younger end of her usual age range. What were they, six when she started watching them? Then they turned seven. Or they might have been eight? She found it difficult to keep up with the ages of children. They grew so much faster than adults, or else the differences between their years were much wider, or else she just didn't care enough to closely keep track. It seemed to always be one of her charges' birthdays, or one of their friends' birthdays, and she was always taking them to a party and humoring them with questions like, How does it feel to be nine?

She had not grown up celebrating birthdays. Every day, you got older. Every minute. Why pick one arbitrary day to commemorate that basic fact of personhood?

When she had to babysit, she preferred to babysit for single-child households. She did not like siblings, and she asked a big up-charge for them. She hated sisters. Twin sisters were the worst of all. And yet, here she was.

She found it hard to look at them. The blatant fact of their sisterhood so apparent on their identical faces. She'd try to put the girls to bed early and ignore it when she heard them talking about her and mimicking her late into the night. She tried to hide her accent by laughing breathily when she spoke, but she wasn't sure this was working.

Tonight, she was babysitting just the one twin while the other twin and her father were at the hospital. She was not sure if the girl would make it. There'd been an accident at the pool. The neighbor who called her had not told her very much, and for once, she felt the pressure of someone else's silence. It made her uneasy too, the silence on the phone. Perhaps this meant she was assimilating.

At the house, the twin she was watching had slept. Immediately. Hard. "Slept like a rock." She knew that idiom but hadn't realized how apt it could be until she saw it. The girl had been standing in front of the couch and then she was lying down on it, sinking into the overstuffed cushions, belly rising and falling, completely and deeply asleep.

She would not bother the girl.

When she'd lost her own sisters, she had not slept more than an hour any one night for weeks. Months maybe. She'd run away and slept on actual rocks for several nights as she escaped.

She felt her foreignness in the most surprising ways sometimes. In the most trivial details. Rock, paper, scissors, for instance. That was a game the girls used to make decisions. She knew a version called grass, rain, bark.

"That doesn't make any sense," they'd complained. "Why would grass beat rain?"

It made sense to her, but she couldn't explain it.

She asked, "Well, why would paper beat rock?"

And they couldn't explain that either.

She did not know when the father would return. She'd stay as long as she needed to. Of course she would. But it was difficult. She was intruding on another family's tragedy and reliving her own and finding it, quite honestly, hard to breathe in the house.

She stayed awake, watching the girl sleep for hours. Trying to hypnotize herself with the girl's even breathing: belly rising, belly falling.

But she was remembering her sisters and how blue their faces were at the end. She was thinking of how this little girl would survive her sister and feel the pain of surviving, as she herself had. As she herself still did.

At sunrise, she slipped into the garage to get a bottle of water. This was the kind of house where you could find two dozen bottled waters lined up in the garage. She hadn't grown up in a house like that, but this neighborhood was full of houses like that. A convenience when there wasn't an emergency, and in case of an emergency, they'd have the supplies. The irony of this wasn't lost on her. Keeping water in case of emergency when, twice for this family, water *was* the emergency.

We never really know the right things to fear. She let this thought ring in her head for a moment.

She was framed by a car on her left and a wall on her right and two bicycles in front of her. They did not have training wheels. She was impressed by that. Everything in the garage was the color of dust. It was dark and damp and her lungs were thankful for it, the wet air. She felt reptilian. Like an ancient organism. The girl was sleeping, so she could stay there in the garage and breathe for a while.

She sat on the garage floor, back against the door to the house, drinking her water. She thought of the woman at the refugee organization who'd interviewed her. The woman's patience as she'd gone on and on, telling her story for hours. And that small act of kindness: the woman giving her a glass of cold water. She'd wanted to weep when she drank it.

An hour passed. Two. The babysitter was thinking of nothing, finally. Some ideas for possible art shows, percolating gently in the back of her mind. She had rooms in herself the way a house did. A house like this. The garage of herself with lots of damp, dark things she wouldn't want brought inside the home: fears in boxes that were mislabeled, memories vacuum-sealed in small containers as if they could stay there, airtight.

She took out her keys and began scraping them against her legs. The dull feeling of it was something less than pain and she wanted to feel something sharper. She began to bite her fingernails, absentmindedly, piling the little crescents in her lap. How many pieces of her body could she collect right here?

When the door opened, she nearly fell backward. She jumped up at the base of the stairs, turning. The girl was there above her, angry and frazzled. Covered in bandages.

"Ouch!" exclaimed one on her forehead.

"Whoops!" yelled the one on her cheek.

"Uh-oh!" shouted the one that ran down the bridge of her nose.

What the fuck, the babysitter thought. What the fuck happened? She pulled her cardigan tighter but otherwise did not move. There was no blood anywhere.

"You were nowhere!" the girl cried. "I couldn't find you!" She leapt down the two stairs toward the babysitter. She hit the babysitter on the chest and shoulders with her small fists. The babysitter was not sure the girl had touched her before. She stopped the girl's fists and held one of them inside her own two hands as if capturing a butterfly.

"Hey," she whispered.

"You were nowhere!" The girl was still screaming but slower, and her arms stopped punching. "Why did you do that? I couldn't find you! Where did you go?"

And because the babysitter could not stand to look into the girl's eyes—not now that she might be newly sisterless, like herself—she pushed the child's head onto her shoulder.

She hugged the girl. The girl hugged back. They breathed and kept breathing, and neither one of them cried.

THE ICE IN THE tray was gray and cloudy. Lionel wished it were clear. Maybe the crystal cubes could show him the future, he would like that, or even the past. No, especially the past.

All right, he thought, sipping a glass of fruit punch. A pink stain emerged over his lip. He could feel it there, wet and cold, and the feeling reminded him of the mustache he'd lost long ago. All right, he thought again. He sighed and looked around.

He had dismissed the babysitter a half hour ago. "What do I owe?" he asked at the door as if she had just pumped his car full of gas or something equally impersonal. The babysitter was too young and too awkward to say anything about his daughter or ask about her condition. She just gave him a dollar amount and looked at his shoulder, away from his face. He used to feel sad for this babysitter, so obviously foreign, so obviously alone and strange. He had a hard time understanding her accent, but the girls did okay with it. Right then, he could see that she was feeling sad for him and he felt a little repulsed by the reversal.

"She'll be okay," he said, too confidently.

The girl exhaled. "I'm so glad," she said.

"I mean," he needed to clarify, "I hope that she will."

"Oh," she said, "me too." She looked at him oddly.

How to end this conversation? They couldn't very well say, "Have a good one."

"See you recently," she came up with, and quickly corrected herself. "*Soon*. I mean, see you soon. I always get that wrong." Her face scrunched, embarrassed.

He stood at the sink, trying to make himself move. It was early morning. He'd go back to the hospital in a few hours.

In the sink, dishes were piled up, and there was a murky sea of stopped-up water, the detritus of two half-eaten meals. He noticed a smell in the kitchen.

"Wash them," he instructed himself. "Put them away." Only, it was not his own voice; it was the voice of his late wife. He'd heard her in his head many times, but she'd never spoken through him like that.

The top plate was smeared with peanut butter over an image of a cartoon princess, his daughter's favorite plate. But which daughter? He could not say for certain. Below this plate, a child's fork, about as big as an oyster fork, with a polka-dot handle and something greenish brown and unidentifiable on the end of a tine. He submerged an arm up to an elbow and reclaimed more pieces. The small plastic dishes of children. Cups with handles on both sides. A cereal bowl with an attached straw for sucking up the sugary milk.

Each time he resurfaced from the ocean of food waste, there was a soft clamor of shifting plasticware. It held none of the tension of wineglasses or china or things that might break. Yet it did betray a fragility.

Wash them. Naomi's voice spoke through him again. *Put them away.*

Was he going crazy? Or had he been crazy his whole life?

Put away childish things.

This was a refrain from a song he had known but forgotten. Childish things. Where was that line from? The Bible, originally, but taken up by that musician: Skip. What had happened to that musician? Had he had only that one song?

Naomi would have known.

"What happened to Skip?" he tried asking her. He said the question out loud, startling himself with the volume of his voice, which he had trouble controlling.

But the Naomi in his head said nothing. There was a cold, solid silence.

Scenes from the hospital replayed in his head. At least . . . he kept thinking before stopping himself because what was the bright side? He couldn't find any. It was an old habit. Naomi used to refer to it as his "relentless and offensive optimism."

In Lionel's own defense, he didn't *want* to be a hopeless optimist. He just detested self-pity. That was what he liked to think. He had never been one to dwell on unanswerable questions, like, Why did bad things keep happening to him?

He liked to believe that he took things in stride. But this was not the case either. It was more that he accommodated whatever befell him. He had become the kind of man who lost his wife to the sea and then nearly lost a daughter to the water also.

Poor Lionel. Poor Naomi. Poor Maeve.

On his drive home, the car radio had played an endless stream of eerie advertisements. Had the world ended? It seemed so.

"Ciel-it to protect your house from sinkholes."

"The Revelation Mask. It's a whole new kind of gas mask."

"Prosyntus. Make age just a number."

That last one, Prosyntus, was developed by the company where his wife had worked as a researcher, a job she had hated.

"I don't want to live in a world where rich people stop their bodies from aging but where poor people get murdered by governments and nobody cares."

What was she referring to? he wondered. In any case, he thought, at least she didn't live in that world anymore.

IN THE GIRL'S BEDROOM, a window was opened, curtains were parted, and a switch was turned: light.

"Isn't she cold?" a neighbor asked.

The girl's body temperature was being carefully maintained by blankets and warm IV fluids. Nonetheless, once the image of a cold child was evoked, it was allowed to hang suspended for only a second before the window was, once again, closed.

In the days since the girl was returned to the Wilhelms' house, the neighbors had assembled a meal train and a shared procedure for tending to her. They'd arrive with some kind of freezable dinner, they'd dust or scrub or vacuum for an hour, they'd stand over the girl for twenty or thirty minutes, they'd take their dish from the drying rack and leave. They felt drawn to visit out of a common mix of feelings. It included neighborly obligation, pity, and morbid curiosity.

They knew that the girl was not sleeping, technically, but they had not vacuumed in her bedroom, for they had not wanted to call attention to her wakelessness and they found it vaguely distasteful that they should interrupt the site of this spectacular tragedy with a device so loud and banal.

Because of this, a moth had laid eggs in the unvacuumed carpet fibers below the girl's bed.

As they watched the girl, the same thought pulsed through the neighbors' minds. It was not a prayer. It was just something they wanted to remember.

(You are awake, they told themselves.)

Sometimes they'd discreetly pinch their upper arm or the loose skin between their thumb and index finger so that they could feel that pain and—with it—their own states of relative consciousness.

(You are awake. You are awake.)

On rare occasions, the twin emerged.

They saw the twin so infrequently they'd manage to forget a twin existed and lived in the house, so there was the recurring shock of it—the girl, awake and peeling open a bruised banana, or else awake and eating pastel-colored cereal from a plastic bowl, or else awake and blowing her nose into her pajama sleeve, which would disgust them under usual circumstances. They shook their heads, swallowed, braced themselves, and the girl sighed dramatically.

"I'm not her, remember?" the twin said.

Yes, right. How could they keep forgetting? They'd return to slicing up a meat lasagna to fit inside the quickly overcrowding freezer.

The neighbors were not the only visitors. Doctors and nurses came through twice each day to record any changes to the girl's status, but there were no changes to the girl's status.

She remained in her strange state, inexplicably continuing to breathe unaided. The doctors and nurses expected that at any moment, her breathing would stop. They had tried to impress this upon the girl's father.

The girl's father was not sure he believed them. Though he was a scientist, he was also the type of man who could find a thin thread of hope in the most dire and desperate situation.

The twins breathed in and out at the same pace and tempo as they always had. The very first time the father held the girls, one infant crooked in each arm, he noticed this.

It continued: their synchronized breathing.

Their bellies rose and fell at the same time, their breaths taken and given, taken and given, in their two sets of lungs, in unison.

–11–

A QUARTER CENTURY OF SLEEP

"TIME OCCURS AT VARYING SIZES AND SCOPES, BUT tectonic plates move at the same rate fingernails grow."

The audience begins reciting their litany and Luke does not need to look at the program; he has learned it by heart.

He finds this funny, in a dark way. That his mind isn't broken completely. That instead, it is broken only in the ways that matter the most.

It was an unlikely decision, all those years ago when he chose to have the procedure. He was the youngest to have it and he wouldn't have been able to afford it, but Genesix had been a client so they gave him a deal.

He had Prosyntus for one main reason: to preserve the person he'd been with Tess. He remembers deeply disliking the person he was becoming without her. He didn't want to confront that person in the mirror, day after day for the rest of his life.

He had a single injection and he forgot the entirety of Tess's existence.

He likes to laugh at that irony. He wonders if Tess was the kind of person who would have laughed at it too.

"Time is the indefinite progress of existence. It continues with and without us, but without us for much longer."

The litany is a list of how time operates. It reminds him of Tess's notebooks of lists.

Luke knows that among the Congregants, he is lucky—Tess kept lists and he took photographs, and so he has a record of his time with her.

Still, that record is artificial—he isn't *remembering* when he reads her lists or looks at his photographs. It's more like reading someone else's story.

It's like the archive they will be making today. Luke wonders if the other Congregants see it this way. How, when you curate the past, you change it. The story you tell becomes the story that's told and everything untold is lost. It's better than having no story at all, he supposes.

He has a thousand photographs of Tess. In the years after the procedure, he could stay awake all night poring through them. But there was more to her than he'd been able to capture. He came to stare at the negative space that surrounded her in every photograph. Over time, that was all he could see.

There is one picture of her in a diner where she has mustard on her chin, for instance. She looks so sad to him even though she's flashing him a gorgeous smile. He can't even look at that photo anymore.

There is only one photograph that feels true and complete. This is the one he brought along today. The picture he wants to leave with the sleeping child inside the caves.

It belongs to her, to the sleeping child. After all, she is in the picture too.

"Time is a piece of dust landing in a girl's left eye while she is riding a bicycle."

When he first joined the Congregants, all he knew was that the sleeping child was the girl in his photo—the girl in the blue hat, sitting next to Tess on a bench in a cemetery. Neither Tess nor the girl was looking at him and he felt they might not have known he was there.

When he read the news and saw that people were praying to this girl, he went to Jacob's Circle just to see her himself.

He waited on the front lawn and, finally, he stood beside her bed and he breathed along with her. And that was when he recovered a single, solid memory of his late wife.

He had breathed just like this, he remembered, silent and in reverence.

They had stood in front of a wide-open space. He and Tess and a beautiful dog. He couldn't say whose dog it was. He remembered that he had kept breathing and he had felt the joy of that: being there, breathing, with Tess.

The clarity of this memory felt like the end of a bad headache. When his five minutes ended and he returned to the chapel, he never told anyone about his recovered memory. But the sleeping child had made him remember, and that was why he stayed with the Congregants. He kept hoping he might remember again.

"Time fills every inhale and every exhale and the moments between inhales and exhales so that even the gaps of time are filled with time."

Luke did have one other memory return in his time with the Congregants, but it was not something he was proud of, and Tess wasn't in the recollection.

He remembered this: a humid evening, a long bike ride, feeling sweaty and anxious loitering in a parking lot. And then there she was, the sleeping child's mother—he remembers her name tag, Dr. Naomi Wilhelm, and how he yelled at her. About what? About Tess? He was furious. The mother was smoking a cigarette. He kept staring at her name tag as he yelled, and weirdly, he cried in heaving sobs, like a roil of pressure unleashed.

Dr. Wilhelm was entirely unfazed by his outburst. She did not try to console him and she left him there, crying, alone.

Why had they both been so angry?

This is not a detail he has forgotten. He remembers vividly that he never understood why.

-12-

Eight years before Maeve's sleep

ON THE ISLAND OF PALMAVJA, ON AN OVERCAST AFTERnoon, a girl who would become a famous performance artist took a shortcut. She was with her sisters in the garment district, and they were on their way to the tailor and not in any real hurry. She began to see that the vacant lot they were cutting through had transformed into an open-air drug market. The girl lingered behind the others, taking it in. Next to a store that once sold very soft denim, a man approached her.

At first, she did not recognize the man and she tensed. He had a crooked body, joints and limbs pointing out at strange, sharp angles. There was a tie knotted around the collar of his wrinkled button-up shirt. The tie was brown and striped with a pattern of bookshelves on it. Upon seeing the tie, she reconsidered the face, and its features arranged into those of her former teacher: Mr. V.

She breathed. The hinge of her jaw relaxed and she smiled. She was about to say hello, but just then, an officer appeared and placed the teacher under arrest.

Someone grabbed her arm—her older sister.

"Come on," her sister whispered, and they took off running along with the others toward an abandoned van missing both its front doors. The sisters crawled in and crouched low in the front seats while officers descended and raided the lot.

And so her first image of the epidemic on Palmavja was this: Mr. V. and his transformed body. His bone-thin wrists hanging loosely in the bright cuffs meant to restrain him, his crusted eyelids fluttering closed as he shook his head, the sweat gluing his hair to his skin, which was bluish but for a rosebud of lesions blooming at the corner of his mouth in a pulsing blood red.

This same mouth on this same teacher used to tell stories, old folktales. As he sat atop his desk, he'd issue, in a warm baritone, three words to quell their classroom of rowdy children. It was almost like magic when he did that.

"Ladies and gentlemen," he used to say, reminding them of what they were not yet but were meant to become.

In the gray light of the vacant lot, as the officer pushed Mr. V. with the pad of a fingertip—afraid, perhaps, to make too much contact and catch what was, once again, spreading—and as that touch on his concave chest made the teacher move backward one step and another and a third, folding him into the officer's vehicle, and as the officer—needlessly—hit the back of Mr. V.'s skull with his club, she kept watching, rapt.

Even when her sisters shielded their eyes and tucked their heads to make themselves smaller, she did not look away. First, she watched through the streaky windshield of the van she hid inside, then also through the untinted window of the officer's car. And the effect of that—window on window, glass over glass—made her feel . . . what?

Later, when she was interviewed at the refugee center and she told this story the one and only time she told it to anyone, she would struggle to accurately describe this particular sensation. Finally, she'd land on these descriptions: it made her feel like she was seeing her life through the small end of a set of binoculars, she'd say, or else peering into a display case inside a display case inside a museum.

At this, the woman who was conducting the interview paused. She'd been holding a notebook but had taken no notes. Now, she flipped to a new page and wrote something down.

THE PALMAVJA THE SISTERS knew was a dull and lusterless island. They grew up in a flat-edged world, knowing nothing of the country's past of pain and addiction. This was not their fault but it was not by accident either; on the island of Palmavja, the history of briar palm had been buried.

It was only after she arrived on the shore of a new country and began learning a new language that she discovered it. She found a book about the purpose of pain in human society with a long chapter about Palmavja. She read it so often, she had parts memorized.

At the refugee center, she retold this story to the woman as well.

The earliest evidence of briar palm came from her own ancestors' artifacts in the northern part of the island: mortars and pestles and drinking urns. Since the plant's leaves were toxic, the indigenous tribes would follow intricate processes passed down orally, crushing it into a topical lotion that could ease stiff joints, and boiling it into a tea that had a pleasant narcotic and analgesic effect.

In such forms, it would have been no more addictive than coffee.

The practice of smoking briar palm started much later. It was introduced by colonists, and because it was so profitable and so addictive, the imperial government formed a joint-stock company and traded the processed briar palm mainly to the northern tribes.

In time, the tribal chiefs banned the substance, a move that sparked a series of armed conflicts with the colonists known, outside the island, as the Three Palmavja Wars.

What were the wars called on the island? the woman at the refugee center asked.

On the island, she said, the wars were not known at all.

A GENERATION BEFORE HER birth, Palmavja suffered several massive earthquakes and an economic depression, and then briar palm began blooming again.

At that time, the country was led by a dictator.

The drug derived from the plant was intravenous and even more potent. When the dictator's son died from an overdose, he targeted the ethnic minority in a campaign against drugs that was, really, a genocide.

Military police were sent to the villages. There were bloody protests and riots and war crimes. This ended only when briar palm itself disappeared.

The dictator was overthrown, time passed, and the island was said to pass into new times.

The first president of Palmavja gave the country a new official name with the word "Republic" in it. She promised that the children and children's children would know nothing of the sharpness of needles and that those who had known such things would find no reminder, no temptation, to know such things again. That was the impetus for a massive redesign. It created hordes of jobs and the economy recovered so people thought that yes, there was hope.

Anything that once shined was given a matte finish in shades like eggshell and unbleached linen. Glittering was considered outdated and garish. All points were filed to bluntness. All corners made round.

Even paper thickened to fit this prevailing aesthetic. A material had been synthesized that was heftier, so all books contained heavy, cream-colored pages that made a satisfying clacking when turned. The original meaning of the word "paper cut" was lost.

She and her sisters knew the phrase as a swear one might whisper below one's breath after a small preventable accident.

What kinds of accidents? asked the woman at the refugee center.

Like hitting your elbow or stubbing your toe.

BY THE TIME SHE was born, nearly nothing remained of those earlier times.

There were the faintest traces: a nursery rhyme that warned of a monster with rosebuds at his elbows, whose skin was tinged blue. That monster, like all childhood monsters, was assumed to be invented and not based on any historical fact.

Otherwise, the only glimpse she'd had into the past came from Mr. V. He had taught her many things—basic economics, the parts of the brain and what each was responsible for: senses, memory, pleasure, pain. But the best was when he told them folktales from the old Palmavja.

There was a tale of butterflies flying off in formation. A myth of a tribe of ancient people who swam to new shores. There were stories of spindles too. In her favorite, a princess was cursed to prick her finger and die. The king issued an order: all spindles had to be burned.

But you can't fool a curse, Mr. V. would say.

Once, there were four sisters who grew up on an island together.

In her lengthy interview, she had finally reached the part where she entered the story.

Each sister had tiny ears and a mole at the corner of her mouth. The moles were orbs of different shades and sizes and she thought of them like planets from the same solar system. They lived with their father whom they competed to love and who loved them each the same.

They shared very few things: their father, their same ears, their moles. But aside from that—the ears, the moles, the love—they were different.

Each sister was, within herself, many sisters. For instance, the sister who preferred sunrise to sunset was also the sister who would not drink cow's milk. And the sister who always went barefoot was also the sister who was a skilled swimmer but detested the ocean because the salt stung. Meanwhile, the sister who first fell in love with a man was also the sister who would paint inanimate objects. The dented washbasin that held their laundry, the silver candlesticks with tall flames, the kitchen window with its thick blue curtain, the hats that stacked up together by the front door.

All the sisters loved to tell stories. And all their stories began with the same single word, which rooted them firmly in the past: "Once."

The sisters were seventeen, sixteen, fourteen, and thirteen when the new epidemic started. They had no desire to rebel or anything to rebel against. They loved their father and each other, and they earned high marks in school.

When the rumors began, the sisters heard them like everyone heard them. And if they retold them and helped to spread them, it was because the rumors made for very good stories.

The rumors had to do with old objects. There were turntables with a stylus that could read grooves to play music. There were pens that you dipped in a well to write in a continuous bleed. There were scissors and tweezers and awls and pins.

The stylus on the record was sharp, and the pen was sharp and sucked ink through what were called "capillaries," and even though there were no records to play or thin paper to write on, and so these tools were particularly useless, the sharpness gave the possibility of depth to their whole flattened world.

At parties, a stylus or needle or pen might appear and they would line up with outstretched fingers to touch it, one by one, that single, sharp thing. This sensation of piercing—they had no word for it, so they made up new words. When adults heard the teenagers speak their slang, they felt a hot dread.

Spindles were spoken of, though no one had found any. But there were stories of spindles, and the sisters remembered them.

In the absence of actual spindles, these stories gave power to the keepers and tellers of them. There was flax spun into gold, thread woven through a labyrinth, a spinning wheel made to sing.

When the drug reemerged, as some would later feel it was bound to, it had a new look and a new name. Soon it was thrust upon everyone as a cure for everything and doctors were rewarded for prescribing it. Because all references to and artifacts from the previous epidemics had been hidden, nobody thought to fear the new drug until it was too late.

It *did* fit in perfectly. It was a chalk-white ingestible oval. Round and lusterless. No injection. No puncture. No pain.

AFTER SHE LEFT PALMAVJA, she read the book by a historian named Abraham Price and she came to see how this pill was a small part of a very long history.

At the time, though, it was youth culture that was vilified because of the rediscovered antiques. There were political cartoons, public service announcements, and after-school specials about them. There was amnesty offered for anyone who turned one in. Teens were arrested for having puncture wounds on their fingers, for having what looked like tattoos but were only, at first, designs drawn on the skin's surface.

To this younger generation, it was absurd. No one had told them their history, so some did start etching into their skin in typically invisible places: an arrowhead on a hip bone, a pair of scissors on the sole of a foot. These were thought to be gang symbols. Others began to pick away at their bodies, made curious and then defiant by the taboo of it. They used tweezers to pluck out arm hairs, scissors to trim their nails short. It became trendy to have hairless arms and legs, to have no eyebrows.

Even after they saw Mr. V. in the vacant lot—his pointed, emaciated limbs already a violation of the blunt roundedness of the country they'd known—the sisters kept telling stories of spindles, and not always in hushed tones.

A crisis was upon them, but they felt safe from it a while longer yet. They kept going to parties, and nothing bad happened.

The more nothing bad happened, the more it seemed like nothing bad ever would.

BUT MAYBE ONE AFTERNOON, the youngest sister rolled an ankle on the curb of a sidewalk on her way home from school.

Maybe she walked on crutches and her usually dainty ankle swelled up as thick as her thigh.

"Does it hurt?" Maybe her sisters asked her that, massaging it gently.

Maybe she shrugged and said, "Barely," and told them her armpits hurt worse from where the crutches dug in.

Maybe a doctor examined her and said that, thankfully, it wasn't a very bad sprain. But maybe he prescribed her a painkiller anyway. And maybe the pill was dry and hard to swallow, and maybe she had to take two big gulps to get it down.

It could have been like that. A rolled ankle. It could have been almost anything, a toothache, a tonsillectomy, a fractured thumb.

Whatever it was, she would not speak of it.

Not at the refugee center as she was interviewed by that kind, patient woman. When she came to what felt like an end to the story, finally, that woman stood and gave them each a glass of cold water and they drank it in silence together. It was the most generous gift—a glass of cold water and silence. And she was touched by it.

Not when, with that same woman's help, she found an attic apartment in a beautiful suburb where she had enough space for an art studio.

Not the next summer, either, when algae began washing up on the private beach. She knew it could not be briar palm—but still, she would worry, what if it was?

And not even as she began to make art from all the untold stories.

She built herself a new life. She changed her name. Her first shows were well received. She became famous almost overnight. She started dating a pop star and there were rumors of an engagement, a secret marriage. A few months later, they broke up. A tabloid reporter tried to dig up her past.

A new procedure became available and celebrities rushed to get it. It blocked aging and pain through a monthly injection. It gave her an eerie premonition. Why did people have to inflict one pain to stop another?

The tabloid reporter kept trying until she was successful, so the past was exposed and everyone learned where she had come from and what had happened to her. She couldn't care less about that, really, except that she could not make art anymore.

She had no more art left.

Her ex had the procedure and died in a matter of weeks and she thought: Oh, here it is again, isn't it?

She issued a statement warning against the procedure, but it was vague and nobody listened.

And then, day by day, she found herself drawn to it.

Why?

You can't fool a curse, her teacher had said.

Maybe she just wanted to feel what her sisters had felt.

BACK ON PALMAVJA, BY the time the government admitted that the new pill was highly addictive, and by the time the foreign biotech firm that manufactured and marketed it had left the island, thousands were dead and thousands more dying. There were other truths that might have followed this one truth, but they'd stay buried a while longer.

That autumn, the soil froze early. There was a photograph of a public cemetery distributed widely by protesters. She took almost six dozen copies of that photograph with her and nearly nothing else when she left for Marks Island.

In the photograph, rows and rows of fresh graves remained open in a winter landscape. Snow dusted the bluish bodies lying faceup, monstrous—uncovered, unsleeping—in cold beds of dirt.

Monique Gray, the Performance Artist Everyone Wants a Piece Of

MARKS ISLAND BULLETIN | ARTS & CULTURE

The performance artist Monique Gray is a well-constructed enigma. Of her past, almost nothing is known beyond the basic origin story: that she arrived in Marks Island City, alone, as a refugee.

These days, Gray is something of a hybrid: half artist, half celebrity, frequently spotted at red carpet events and movie screenings, beside directors and actors and public intellectuals.

Of her art, she has explained very little, putting forth only brief public statements.

In Gray's first show, *Final Resting Place*, she filled the Siegler Gallery with 50 coffins. There were all types: fairy-tale glass coffins, handcrafted wood coffins, state-of-the-art coffins lined with plush pink velvet. Gray had the lids removed so that the coffins remained open, and the audience was invited to choose one and climb inside. Gray herself spent the show walking through the gallery, standing over each coffin in turn and peering in.

Perhaps most famously, in *Unnamed Sisters*, Gray underwent 48 hours of plastic surgery with no anesthetic. She had her face redone to resemble the faces of three other women, and then had a final surgery to reverse it so that she ended with her original face. Her trademark mole was untouched throughout this process. Tickets to this one-time show started in the tens of thousands, and it was reported that she donated all proceeds, although she has never confirmed this or specified which causes or organizations that money went to support.

Recollection I is her newest work. It includes hundreds of plastic bags filled with the artist's own body parts, collected over the last who-knows-how-many years. The parts are unlabeled. They are, one can guess, her toenail clippings, her skin shavings, her earwax, her tooth plaque, her armpit hair, her leg hair, her pubic hair, her eyebrow hair, her eyelashes, hardened balls of her phlegm, hair that fell or was plucked from her scalp, her scalp, which appears flaked off in large, even pieces as if by a cheese grater, and so on.

This collection by itself is impressive. There are enough bags for each evening's audience to take as many as they wish and do whatever they wish with the contents.

And this is exactly what she asks of her audience. They build and destroy, incorporate and reincorporate.

All the while, the artist herself walks through the gallery naked. With various sharp objects, she cuts and she scrapes and she plucks to fill yet more of these bags.

As she continues adding more of herself, she circulates through the audience, advising them in their manipulation of her.

"Here is one," Gray can be heard whispering loudly, handing a freshly filled bag to a stranger. "Take it. Do something, anything. Good."

Continued on Page 4

-13-

Seven months into Maeve's sleep

LIONEL'S HAIR WAS STILL THINNING AT ITS GLACIAL pace, strand by strand. He had one age spot, dime-sized and the color of wet tree bark, near his left ear. It was darkening, but again, almost imperceptibly.

Seven months to the day after the accident, the doctors and nurses told Lionel, "There is nothing else we can do," or, more passively, "There is nothing to be done."

Did Lionel understand?

Evangeline stood behind the wall, eavesdropping.

Lionel could be heard to say nothing.

The neighbors—who had maintained their daily visits for these months—stopped their mopping, dusting, and dishwashing to better overhear also. Evangeline held in a sneeze.

The doctors and nurses began giving detailed instructions for how to care for Maeve's body, should Lionel choose to keep caring for it.

"This tubing will bring liquid nutrition into her stomach."

And: "Remember the importance of avoiding infection."

And: "Here. This device can pull out her mucus."

And: "Monitor her breathing. At any moment, still, her breathing could stop."

They said that when this happened, it would be best to let it happen.

"She feels no pain. She feels nothing," they reminded him. "Even when ice water was poured into her ear, she had no response."

In the foyer, the last doctor said a last goodbye.

"Are you sure," the doctor asked, "that this is what's best for her?"

Lionel stood speechless, baffled.

This was when Evangeline revealed herself. She ushered the doctor out and closed the door. Then she took her father's hand and led him back into the kitchen.

The neighbors had resumed their scrubbing and sweeping. Even so, when Lionel saw them—dipping a yellow-gloved hand into sudsy water and mopping the linoleum for the third time in two days and disinfecting the toilet in the guest bathroom that had not been used since the last time it was disinfected—their intrusion was suddenly evident. The cleaning fluid smelled citrusy and stung the sinuses. His eyes began to water. Evangeline forced a polite cough to encourage him.

"Please," Lionel said to no one in particular and, in that way, to everyone. "Please," he said again, "you can leave."

Slowly, the neighbors stood. They found their purses, their sunglasses. One or two of them touched Lionel's shoulder and Evangeline's back in gestures to express their condolences. They slipped their shoes on without tying them. They left the house and would not return.

The father, the twin, and the sleeping child were alone together.

Lionel sold the insect museum that few people visited but that had been, since his wife's death, the sole source of household income. He auctioned off rare insect specimens. He devoted himself to Maeve's care, and otherwise returned to observing the ants in their glass case. He was pleased to record that they belonged to a new generation.

He thought of the original ants as "ant-cestors." He told the pun to Maeve, who kept sleeping. He told the pun to Evangeline, who stared blankly at him and did not even roll her eyes. He told the pun to the ants, who heard it, if at all, as a low vibration through their feet.

Evangeline imagined her own house as a terrarium, Maeve as a very big, very lazy queen. She drew a picture of this with an orange crayon but crumpled it up and threw it in the basket. Secretly, she hoped her father would find it.

She got on her bicycle and rode to the cemetery. There, she took grave rubbings. All of the same grave: her mother's.

She stayed out after sunset and her father never asked her where she went on her bicycle.

When she came back, she knocked on the door, always in the same rhythm. Sets of three: quick, quick, long; quick, quick, long. Like a horse's gallop.

"There you are," Lionel said.

"Here I am," she'd reply.

Periodically, Evangeline amassed too many grave rubbings and the need to dispose of them overcame her. She brought them into her old bedroom late at night and did not look at Maeve, who just lay there, sleeping. She opened the window and let the grave rubbings scatter as she made a wish.

She believed she might have been doing a kind of magic.

One night, bending down to retrieve a dropped crayon, Evangeline discovered the infestation in the carpet below Maeve's bed. The creatures were nocturnal. They were feasting on woolen threads, body oil, sweat, hair.

Evangeline thought these moths had to do with her magic.

Her wish, emphatic and focused and the same each time, was that her twin sister would die.

The house grew dusty, dirty. The living room smelled of leaf litter tracked in on shoes. Of rotten food. Bad breath breathed in and out too many times.

Lionel pulled a chain to turn on the ceiling fan. He thought this would help, but it did not help; it only moved this stench around and around and around.

A NEW CROP OF visitors and again, they came in two factions: medical researchers and people of faith. Both groups had read of the remarkable sleeping child in the news. That she had kept breathing when she should have stopped breathing many months ago.

There were six medical researchers, all men, and they hoped to publish academic articles. They scheduled weekly meetings and collected data from her. They offered a small amount of money in the form of a one-time grant allocation for a few of her qualifying medical expenses.

There were about a dozen people of faith, all old. They hoped to learn something about life and living from the girl.

The people of faith suffered several ailments, physical, spiritual, and otherwise. They had been followers of all kinds of religious denominations, only a few of which were generally considered to be cults. They offered a monthly donation to a fund that they had established in the girl's name.

Lionel appreciated the people of faith. Unlike the doctors and nurses and neighbors and medical researchers, they asked nothing of him. They did not treat his daughter as a specimen. The people of faith wanted to stand silently next to her and breathe for a few minutes on Sundays. To watch her there, sleeping and breathing.

But Evangeline hated them. They were decrepit and smelled strongly of peppermint. They looked at her with tearful expressions. She could tell they felt sorry for her, but she could not have said why.

"Why are they here?" she asked Lionel one afternoon right in front of them.

The people of faith looked at Lionel as if the question were ridiculous, the answer obvious, but they said nothing.

Lionel mumbled, "Shh. For your sister. Shh."

He spoke to Evangeline like this frequently. As though he were trying to put her, also, to sleep.

Night after night, Evangeline sneaked into Maeve's bedroom to watch her creatures. They had encased themselves.

Sometimes, she imagined the moths as her mother—the words were so close, "mother" and "moth," one containing the next. Other times, she imagined the moths as her sister—they, too, were silent and motionless, trapped inside their own bodies.

The medical researchers left. It was abrupt and unceremonious. They had exhausted their limited funding. The people of faith remained, having a renewable resource in faith.

And then, while Lionel was using the handheld vacuum to suck out Maeve's mucus, there was another inexplicable phenomenon.

"Come quick," Lionel told the people of faith who were waiting outside the door.

They came, and they saw it too: hundreds of moths flying out from under the bed. They took on the form of a suspended letter, an *M*.

"Lepidoptera," Lionel called them, not moths.

When the rest of the religious people arrived, Lionel told them the story. He said, "They came from nowhere." He added,

"But nothing comes from nothing," which he meant scientifically, but which was not interpreted that way.

He said it was stunning. That they were bright orange like the carpet fibers they'd been consuming.

He said "awesome," meaning breathtaking.

He said "miraculous," meaning beautiful and strange.

He described the slim odds of so many creatures surviving and developing despite all the cleaning, unseen until the last possible moment. And their formation too. Highly, highly unusual.

Lionel did not tell the people of faith that as he watched the moths swarm from below her, he had a terrible fear and that what he feared, intensely, was that his daughter was about to sprout wings and take flight.

The people of faith believed the moths were a sign. They came to visit more and more. They referred to themselves as Congregants. They told the story of the moths until some details changed, and Lionel did not notice the slight deviations, which would amount to larger ones over time.

Evangeline had found a blue baseball cap on her mother's side of the walk-in closet and hid beneath it. She wore it every day, though it was large on her. She was having trouble sleeping until she stopped sleeping. She was having trouble eating until she stopped eating.

She biked to the cemetery wearing that hat instead of a helmet. She stayed out there later and later each Sunday, and when she returned and knocked that galloping rhythm on the front door—quick, quick, long; quick, quick, long—she resented that she had to come back to this house at all.

Over a breakfast she did not eat she told her father that if Maeve would not die, then maybe she herself could.

Seconds passed. Minutes passed. Hours passed. A few more days and nights passed. All the while: Breaths were taken.

Breaths were given. In unison.

A breeze blew through the window, moving the curtain. The window was closed, the breeze stopped, the curtain stilled.

Lionel made a plan at last.

A car was parked in the driveway. In the living room, a backpack, stuffed too full, was lifted and thrust over a grandfather's shoulder. The backpack was purple with a yellow zipper and looked silly on the old man.

There was a box packed haphazardly by a nine-year-old who did not yet know to put heavy things on the bottom and fragile things at the top. Evangeline lifted the box for a second before she dropped it. There was a noise that sounded like a piggy bank full of coins. It was a jar full of sea glass and a stone.

The grandfather said, "Come on then," and he lifted the box and carried it against his left hip. He took Evangeline's hand, not gently but not unkindly. The brim of her blue hat fell low over her brow.

The grandfather did not say hello to Maeve, who was also his granddaughter.

Evangeline did not say goodbye to Maeve, who would remain, always, her twin. Relief spread down the nape of her neck as she passed her old bedroom and she shivered tremendously, as if shedding a skin.

-14-

A QUARTER CENTURY OF SLEEP

AT THE HEIGHT OF HER CAREER, MONIQUE GRAY WAS known for many things. For producing gruesome works of art that were widely misinterpreted, for being the surviving half of a high-profile—if short-lived—"it" couple, for being a refugee from a violent region who'd tried to hide her past but whose past was exposed.

She abandoned fame and art both once Prosyntus destroyed her memory.

"Time is a puddle of seconds becoming minutes becoming hours, days, weeks, months, years, a lifetime."

She remembers her art, which had to do with her sisters. But she no longer knows how it had to do with them.

In her very first show, which she called *Final Resting Place*, she remembers having a gallery filled with coffins. But she does not remember seeing her sisters in their real-life final resting places. She has a few copies remaining of the now-famous photograph of the Palmavja cemetery, but she does not recognize any of the corpses who stare out at her, and she has spent a great deal of time staring back at them.

She remembers when Prosyntus killed her ex, and she remembers taking a stand against the procedure even before that cause of death was known. She said that it felt cursed—because it did. It reminded her of a curse she'd known. But she has forgotten the curse also.

"No matter how many superficial attempts we make to cheat death," she said on a talk show, "death always wins."

Nobody understood what she had been trying to say. They assumed she just wanted more publicity.

She remembers this too—how, in this country and this city, when you have an audience, everyone wants to watch but nobody listens.

"Time is the loneliness of all the world's sleep through all the world's history."

Of course, it didn't help that one week after that talk show appearance, she had the procedure. Why did she have it?

She remembers being lowered in a chair by a nurse whose ears stuck out from his mask, having her skin pricked with a needle, and sleep.

Of her sisters, there's almost nothing. Just the thought that when they died, it felt like she'd swallowed a tangle of thorns. But what did *that* feel like? A tangle of thorns in one's throat? She has no memory of this kind of pain.

Inside her handbag, she has her copy of a book about the role of pain in society. There is a whole section about Palmavja that she must have read a thousand times. It has her highlighting and notes filling the margins. She would be happy if she could forget that history, but she does not want that history to *be* forgotten. That is why she has brought the book to be part of the archive.

Monique has never told this to anyone, but one other thing she remembers: the house of the sleeping child; in fact, all the houses of that gated neighborhood where she lived when she first arrived. She remembers the attic apartment of the house that would later serve as the chapel.

She lived there in that stretch when her days were spent watching bad movies to learn the language, finding work as, of all things, a babysitter to support herself as she began to make art.

Maeve wasn't always a very nice girl. She could be cruel, as all little girls can be. She'd made fun of her accent and her mole. Monique remembers being just lonely enough and young enough and sisterless enough at that time to feel bad about this—teasing from an eight-year-old.

In her memory, the girl had a sister who was in all ways identical to her. She knows that this is not accurate. It's how she discovered that her imagination has leaked into the gaps of recollection and filled them in incorrectly. It has to be her own sisters she is trying and failing, trying and failing to remember.

Nonetheless, Monique loves this specific false memory of a little ghost girl. She's been chasing this vision for over a decade.

She can remember all kinds of things about the child that her mind has invented for her, like the cycling punches of the sister's fists when she threw a tantrum, and the smell of the sister's scalp when she held her, still tantruming, tight to her chest.

"Time is the force of wind and sand and waves against a shard of glass, dulling it, until it is found on a beach by a child who brings it home and places it inside a glass jar that, too, will find its way to the ocean and be dulled down by the force of wind and sand and waves. Time is this endless cycle of glass into ocean into glass into ocean into glass again."

–15–

A decade into Maeve's sleep

EVERY THURSDAY, LIONEL TRIMMED MAEVE'S FINGERnails and toenails. He had opted to keep her hair long. He washed and combed it and let it spill out below her head to fall onto the floor.

He mostly ignored the protest signs on his neighbors' lawns and the new petition about his daughter and her followers. He turned Maeve's body every eight to ten hours so that she would not develop bedsores. Each time he did so, he knocked softly against the nightstand in a set of three to create an old rhythm: quick, quick, long; quick, quick, long. Like a horse's gallop. He thought of Evangeline coming home when he did this. He believed he was only remembering the past and not, also, imagining any hoped-for future of her return.

EVANGELINE HAD BEEN FOLLOWING the story of her twin sister. She had learned all about the complaints in the neighborhood along with the newest miracle of her followers.

There had been, by the accounts, three miracles.

In the beginning, it was simply that Maeve had kept breathing. Almost a year after the accident, there were hundreds of moths born beside her in an instant.

When those two events occurred, Evangeline had still been living in the house. But now, now that she had spent more of her life without her twin, there was a new miracle.

Maeve had fallen into her sleeping state at the age of eight. By eighteen, she should have undergone a complete metamorphosis from child to teen. But though her hair and nails kept growing, the rest of her remained untouched by time.

The procedure to end aging had been a disaster and thousands were left with broken promises, broken lives, broken memories. But here was her sister, asleep and unaged; preserved and remembering, somehow still, to breathe.

Once this came out, the Congregants' numbers ballooned.

What did Lionel make of it? A reporter asked him this in the latest article that Evangeline had found. "Is it a miracle?"

Lionel was said to have smiled and shrugged and told the reporter, "I couldn't say."

Evangeline could picture her father precisely in that scene—that shrug, that smile, that noncommittal response.

She had always struggled to find the right words to describe him. The indecisive man who had decided one day to stop raising her.

Maybe nothing could describe him as concisely and accurately as his two passions: astrophysics and insects.

He was incapable of living in and understanding the human world.

LIONEL USED TO THINK that caring for a sleeping child for a decade had changed him fundamentally. He thought it had fully worn down the hard outer shell that had been his optimism, his old eagerness to believe that the best possible scenario was also the most likely.

Was it a miracle? the reporter had asked him.

He couldn't say. He really could not.

There were, he felt, several equally likely explanations. He had believed that he was capable of holding all these possibilities in his mind and feeling a compassionate nonattachment. He had thought Maeve had taught him this.

For instance: It might be a miracle. And it might not be.

Maeve might wake up. And she might keep sleeping.

Naomi may have intended to kill herself. And she may have drowned by accident.

Evangeline might yet come home. And she might stay away.

But then Evangeline had sent him a letter.

It was her final question on the list of questions that pinched at him, shaking his confidence in his own agnosticism.

When he thought of all the possible answers and outcomes, he liked to imagine each as a string—in the cosmic sense, like string theory—one-dimensional, theoretical. But at the other end of them—he could not help it now, since reading her letter—he had started to picture some greater power, pulling and spinning those strings.

And what was *that* if not, after everything, the highest form of optimism: faith?

"I WANT TO BE dead." That was what she'd said to her father about a year after her sister began sleeping.

Or was it, "I want to die"? Or, "I'd be better off dead"?

Something like that.

She'd made a suicidal declaration and there was the history of her mother to contend with and so her father had sent her away.

It had been nine years since she'd seen him. Nine years since she'd spoken to him. Nine years of living in a city only a few miles south of the suburb where the silent, sleeping version of herself remained.

She had spent those years with her grandfather, her father's father, who was a completely different kind of person from his son: Stern. Logical.

"If you don't want to talk to him, you don't have to talk to him," her grandfather said. This was early on in their new life together. "It's that simple."

"I don't want to talk to him," she'd replied. She hadn't needed to think it over.

"Fine," he said. That had been that.

But seven months ago, just after Maeve came into the news again, Evangeline sent her father a letter. She'd be going away to college soon and she might never see her sister again. She had a kind of premonition about that, which could have just been the clarity of getting older and wanting closure.

She was trying to make sense of some things, she wrote to him. She kept her tone mature and impersonal. She told him to please refer to the enclosed questions.

"I'd appreciate," she wrote, "if you could send me your thoughts."

THE LIST OF QUESTIONS was one page long. Lionel had read it every day since he'd opened it.

There were details about her mother's death that she had been picking at. Like: "Why would she have worn a wet suit to drown herself?"

And her mother's scholarly work, which she'd read but not understood. She attached a press release on Naomi's award-winning research for reference. "In her dissertation," Evangeline wrote, "what did she mean when she described the ancient alga as either briar palm or its 'ecological twin'?"

There were pieces of her own memory that now seemed strange to her: "Why did we spend so much time digging at Rocky Beach?"

If it ended there, it would have been straightforward. He could have told her honestly, "Your mother is the only one who would know."

He wouldn't have doubted anything or felt in any way unmoored by possibilities he hadn't considered.

But there was the last question, which was something he didn't think even Naomi would have been able to answer, and which opened new depths of untold history where his sleeping daughter and his whole splintered family might fit.

"In the Marks Museum of Human History," she wrote, "there's an artifact. He's a tiny doll of an ancient prince that was found in the Caves of Adina. He's asleep but his nails are long, and he's covered in that same red rock she was always having us look for, the same rocks that were in her pockets. Who was that ancient boy and what are those rocks?"

EVANGELINE WAS WATCHING THE Congregants on the news again. They were preparing for their ritual dance on the front lawn of her old home.

Her father had not answered her letter yet. She was beginning to doubt that he would.

On the news, the camera panned to a neighbor's lawn, where there was a protest sign. "Save Maeve," it read, which made Evangeline scoff the way her mother used to scoff at the neighbors.

What it should say, she thought, was, "There goes the neighborhood," or, "No cults in my backyard." Not that she was on the Congregants' side in this debate either.

The first flock of elderly religious folks—the ones she'd known and hated as a little girl—they must have grown old and died and been replaced, one by one, member by member, so that the group was, in effect, a new group. They had a much bigger crowd. Many lived in the house across the street, which they had purchased to use as their chapel.

Up to three times each day, they came out in their winged orange robes—as they were doing now—and performed a dance that was inspired by the formation of moths.

A few of them had taken vows of silence to be closer to Maeve. Most consumed only liquid nutrition, as Maeve did.

Last fall, the group had to formally disavow the practice of inserting feeding tubes because someone had almost died from complications.

They gathered in front of Maeve's bedroom, where the curtains were open and where, now, the news camera zoomed in.

Evangeline looked past her twin at the figure by the bedside: her father.

He was massaging Maeve's wrist and her elbow.

He was looking down at Maeve's collar, which had come off-center. He attempted to fix it, but it would not lie as he wanted it to. All at once, Evangeline felt the urge to cry as she watched her father tend to her twin so carefully.

Outside the bedroom, the Congregants were dancing.

Her father tried to fix Maeve's shirt yet again.

Dr. Naomi Clarke, 27, Awarded Francis Marks Prize for the Ancient Sciences

PRESS RELEASE

The Academy of Paleobiologists, with support from the Alfred G. Siegler Foundation, announces that Dr. Naomi Clarke is the recipient of this year's Francis Marks Prize for the Ancient Sciences. Dr. Clarke, 27, is the youngest recipient of the prize in its 30-year history.

Dr. Clarke is a paleobiologist and archaeologist reconstructing the ecosystem of ancient Marks Island. Along with leading an extensive excavation on Grace Beach, Dr. Clarke has developed a strategy to computationally model the effects of ancient seismic activity on human and marine life. Using evidence from the fossil record and the results of her modeling, she has demonstrated convincingly the presence and prevalence of a unique alga in the region at least 20,000 years ago, but probably much earlier.

Dr. Clarke's theory is based on the extremely high levels of phosphorus that are still detectable in trace minerals from deep in the seabed. She posits that a major earthquake caused both uplifting and burial, moving the minerals to their current location.

These deposits would have released into the water the nutrients necessary to support a long-lasting algae bloom. The alga may have been *Sentis palma* (briar palm), a species now found only near the small island nation of Palmavja, or it might have been similar but distinct, in which case the two types of alga would likely be considered ecological twin species.

Dr. Clarke, who just completed her doctoral degree, is hoping to continue her research and broaden its scope in the years ahead. She plans to expand her modeling and investigate the role that the alga played in both the ecosystem and human life. She hopes it will lead to a greater understanding of the ancient humans of Marks Island.

-16-

Twenty-one months into Maeve's sleep

A FEW DAYS BEFORE THE FOUNDERS DAY GALA, A FIELD trip of third and fourth graders arrived at the museum with a wild little girl. She ran through the exhibits, making a mess of what Kevin had been trying very hard to keep clean.

"Please," he said to the adult in the room, "can you stop her from doing that?"

He had just paused mid-tour to try to stop the girl from smudging her name on a glass display. "She needs to spit her gum out as well."

The chaperone—he saw that the woman was very beautiful. There was a scrawny boy at her side, holding her hand. He had a younger version of her face. The same small nose and round cheeks, but with shorter hair and someone else's eyes.

"I'm sorry," she said, and she did sound sorry. She sighed, and her shoulders moved down her back and he saw how elegant and long her neck was.

"That's okay," Kevin said.

He knelt beside the terror of a girl. He could feel the chaperone watching him.

"Hello," he said. "I'm Mr. Marks. What's your name?"

She didn't say anything. She was working on the smudge mark for a *V*. She had an unruly cowlick.

"I need you to stop making a mess of things." He was trying to be reasonable, but the girl still hadn't stopped what she was doing or even looked at him.

"What would your mother say if she saw you acting like this?" He raised an eyebrow.

She stopped and turned toward him.

"She wouldn't say anything, Mr. Marks, because my mother is dead."

Kevin shivered. Not so much because of what she had said, but because of how she had said it. "My mother is dead." Like it was any regular thing you might tell a person. The weather, a joke.

He looked at the chaperone, who held his gaze now, steadily. She nodded at him, meaning yes, he did have to do something to help this sad, strange little girl. He could do that. He could help a sad child.

"Can I tell you a story?" he asked. She didn't say yes or no, so he just began. He told her the tale of one of his grandfather's findings. The chaperone and all the other children listened in.

This is the story of a prince.

He was found inside the Caves of Adina. Had she been there? No? Well, the class would see the caves in a bit. And did she know that ancient humans lived on this land once, a long, long time ago?

Yes? Okay.

He began walking backward, leading them toward the next exhibit. The girl and her classmates followed. The teacher and the chaperone too.

They were an indigenous people. That means native. And this land, it was an island back then—so we don't know how these people first got here, where they came from. The isthmus—you remember on the bus ride? That long, skinny bit of land you drove over? That's called an isthmus, and—

What does this have to do with the prince?

She was impatient.

The prince, right. We don't know how he survived or what he meant to the people. But we know he must have been very important. Because he was rock, he was not fragile, and even his little crown was still intact when he and the people were found tens of thousands of years later. They took very good care to make sure he wouldn't be ruined by the passing of time. They covered him in red, glowing rocks, like sequins.

Kevin stood so he was blocking the display with his body.

The people in the caves, they were all grown-ups. No children, just grown-ups and one very old man, and this one prince, this little red doll, the size of your forearm. Maybe a bit smaller. It's very possible he was modeled on a real boy who was never recovered.

Kevin moved aside to reveal the display now: a red prince with a crown of beads and a gown of red, glittering rocks. His eyes were closed. His hands rested under his head. The nails on his fingers were long.

"Xumu?" someone whispered, reading the text beside him.

"That's a good story," the girl said in a whisper. She was staring at the red rock, transfixed.

A few children came closer to the display and shouted their questions, and Kevin let the girl make up her own answers to all of them. She did not look away from the prince as she spoke.

"No," he heard her say, "he's not dead. He's just sleeping. One day, he's gonna wake up."

Kevin found the chaperone again while the children ate greasy pizza. He sat beside her and the woman asked about the ancient tribe of Marks Island. She was particularly interested in Papa

Marks, the old man. She said something about divergent evolution, which was wrong so he corrected her, but he didn't think she was really listening.

He learned her name—Sylvia Price—and her son's name—J. P. She worked at the news station and had a husband who was a historian. She seemed distracted the whole time she talked to him, but he still liked talking to her.

Much too soon, the buses were in front of the building and it was time for the class to leave.

"You should come back," Kevin said to Sylvia.

She took her boy's hand and stood up. "We will," she said. Then she asked J. P., "Won't we?" But the boy said nothing and they walked toward the bus.

Kevin was on his way to his office, moving slowly, still thinking about Sylvia, when a little voice called out behind him.

"Mr. Marks," she said. It was the girl. She had lingered behind the others.

"Yes?" he said. He crouched down.

"What happened to Xumu? I mean the real Xumu."

"We don't know," he said. "It's just one of the many mysteries. Go catch up with your class, Miss—" She hadn't told him her name, he realized. "What's your name?" he asked. "Miss . . . ?"

"Wilhelm," she said.

"Here, Miss Wilhelm." He didn't know why he did this. Only that she had stared closely at those rocks, and he was still shaken by how she spoke of her dead mother, and so he gave her the red rock from his pocket.

She held it in two hands. "Thank you," she said before she ran toward the bus.

When he got to his office and sat down at his desk and saw the blue whale on the wall, he heard the girl's voice again in his head: Wilhelm, she had said. Wilhelm. And her mother was dead. Did Dr. Wilhelm have a daughter? No, or . . . had she? He couldn't remember. He pulled the newspaper clipping off the wall and turned it over and scoured the three paragraphs he'd been trying hard not to think about for so long.

"She leaves behind a family."

THE MUSEUM WAS TRANSFORMED for the gala. Uplighting cast an atmospheric glow over the space, and ivory curtains were draped between pillars for warmth and texture. Caterers in black suits passed through with trays of hors d'oeuvres.

Kevin was thanked for his generosity in every speech. Even though all he had done was accept another payment from the Sieglers. He waved at the audience, he hoped humbly. The event photographer had him pose with a Genesix executive. Kevin found the attention uncomfortable.

The keynote speaker was a historian: Abraham Price.

Sylvia's husband, Kevin realized. He was much, much older than Sylvia.

Abraham Price explained that he'd made a study of the history of pain in society and that the discovery of Papa Marks—the ancient old man with the chronic condition—had been of particular importance to him.

He spoke for a long time and Kevin fell in and out of listening. Mostly, he was remembering Sylvia and their short conversation.

Afterward, Kevin thought he might introduce himself to Abraham Price, but there was too big a crowd around each of them. He could not break away.

The excitement around museums lasted for many months, but it must have been fading without Kevin noticing because one day, he woke up and the fanfare was dead. Nobody cared about the history he was curating and the museum was empty once more.

What had happened?

The reanimated woolly mammoths kept dying. But worse than that: Genesix's procedure to end aging had gone terribly wrong. There were previously unknown side effects that emerged. It shortened people's life spans and it erased people's most precious memories.

The Sieglers let their contract run out and they did not renew. They stopped using the beach and they stopped donating.

Alone once more, Kevin felt his dread come back in full.

He slept beside the Caves of Adina, but it no longer helped him. There was a silence that the drilling used to fill, and it kept him awake. So, he'd leave no real mark on the planet, he concluded. What had he done it all for, in the end?

And in the end, he thought, what *had* he done?

At his annual physical, a doctor detected an issue with Kevin's heart. When Kevin returned for a follow-up, he was given a six-month prognosis. He was not yet sixty but might not live to be sixty, he was told.

It had been a small life, he thought, and now, also, a short one.

He spent his numbered days the same way he had spent his days before they were numbered: wandering from wing to wing, telling the same stories to any rare visitors, eating a turkey sandwich on dry wheat bread, a meal that he didn't like but ate just the same.

One night, he rewatched the special anniversary broadcast that had aired before the big Founders Day gala all those years before.

There he was, excited and hopeful, interviewed on the talk show. His dimpled chin bobbing up and down as he spoke.

The host asked who should visit the museum, and he answered, brightly, "Everyone."

He hardly recognized his own smiling face.

At the end, he saw something he'd never seen before. A name flying over the screen with a producer credit: Sylvia Price.

He hadn't thought about her in years.

She may have already been working on this program the day she met him. She may have already known who he was. Why hadn't she said so? He had so enjoyed speaking with her. Though it was a very short conversation. Still. His life could have gone so many other ways than the way it had gone. He felt intolerably sad for himself.

When the sixth month passed and Kevin woke at the start of the seventh month, still alive, he went to work as he always did. He noticed some things he had long ago stopped noticing. The cold gurgle of water from the half-broken water fountain on the second floor (it was very refreshing), and the number of stairs to the east wing (thirty, a nice round number), and an item that had been in the lost and found longer than all other items (a bracelet with a gold letter *T*). Soon enough, he stopped noticing these small things yet again. When that extra month ended, he went back to the doctor.

"What gives?" he said. "I'm still here."

The doctor was unfazed. "Sometimes it takes longer," she said. But she did a few follow-ups. The results came back and she paged through them several times before she told him that either someone had made a mistake or a miracle had happened, but in either case, Kevin would live.

He left the hospital to a cloudless, weatherless day. He squinted in the spring sunlight and started to search for his car, knowing he would drive back to the museum, that his living would be the same as his dying had been. And that this was probably what it meant to be a Kevin.

Just as he thought this, he saw her.

She wore a sleeveless blouse and he saw that the skin on her neck looked like limestone, soft, flaky, and her hair was speckled with grays and blacks, like granite. She was still very beautiful.

"Sylvia?" he said. "Sylvia Price? I'm Kevin Marks." She looked at him, head tilted. "Years ago," he went on, "on your news station, you worked on a broadcast about my museum? We met there once. You were a chaperone? On a field trip?"

"I'm sorry," she said. "I don't remember."

He asked her to lunch and they ate at a café that was once one of those retro diners and he learned that she'd been diagnosed with early dementia. She told him that her mother had also suffered from it. It wasn't bad yet, her illness, she said. It came and went and could be gone for days, weeks even.

At lunch, they said nothing more about medical conditions or health scares. They spoke of their lives. Sylvia did most of the talking. Kevin learned that her son had become an architect and moved out of state. That her husband had passed away. He'd been much older than Sylvia, but his death had still come as a shock. And doesn't it always? he asked, rhetorically.

But she answered. "Yes and no," she said. "He had Prosyntus."

Kevin didn't know what to say to that, so he said something empty. "I'm sorry."

"Abe loved your museum," she told him. "The story of your grandfather and Marks Island. It meant a lot to him, all that history."

So she had a life behind her, Kevin thought, but they might still have a bit of life ahead of them too if they were very lucky.

ONCE, KEVIN BROUGHT SYLVIA to his museum after hours. He told her about his childhood, growing up with Adina, her kitchen and the refrigerator. In his office, she saw the two framed portraits of his famous father and grandfather.

Sylvia laughed. "How can you work with these men staring disapprovingly?"

Kevin tried to see the men as Sylvia did.

"But this whale," she said, pointing to the article, "doesn't it just make you feel wonderfully small?"

He looked at the clipping. He wouldn't have said "wonderfully."

He brought Sylvia to the case that held Xumu. He told her the story of it, though she'd heard it before.

Sylvia looked down at the boy made of rock, lying in his little glass coffin.

"I'd like to hold him," she said.

"Okay," Kevin told her. "Wait here."

He found a pair of gloves and disabled the alarm to open the display. She picked the boy up and cradled him, rocking him back and forth and humming a song.

Standing beside her, Kevin saw himself as if in a snapshot. A memento from a past that never was. They formed a perfect, odd family. Two frail older parents and their tiny red son.

As her illness worsened, he told her stories that were really his memories of his life both before her and with her. He used the third person and she did not recognize the characters. Not the one who was him or the one who was her.

But there were still good moments, even if they were fleeting. On one good day, Kevin came to the nursing home and found her awake in the Days Room. She was sitting at the edge of her favorite armchair and watching a talk show that she used to produce. The host was new, the third or fourth since her retirement. He was a fresh-faced boy with sand-colored hair and dark eyebrows, dressed up in what Kevin thought could very well have been his father's suit.

For a while, people around Kevin had been growing younger. That was what it felt like. He'd talked about that with Sylvia and they'd decided that this was how you knew that you were finally and categorically old. When you seemed to stop growing any older or frailer or smaller altogether. Instead, it felt as though you were staying still while everyone else moved faster and faster. It might be from that distance that he would fade away.

Kevin did not expect Sylvia to recognize the program she was watching. Though there was, he saw, the same channel logo in the bottom right corner: the top half of a clock with gold hands inside it that ticked around and around. That image alone could have been enough to remind her.

"I'm here," he said because he didn't think she had noticed him.

"Shh, Kevin," she answered. "It's my show."

So she did remember. He watched it with her, perched on the arm to give his bad hip some rest.

The news that day went like this: someone somewhere was holding some people hostage, demanding something from someone else; someone else somewhere else was citing an accidental discovery as the most hopeful sign of something to date; something else happened to a child long ago and it was either tragic or a miracle depending on whom you asked about it; and yet, elsewhere, something was merging with something to form the biggest something the world had yet known.

Nothing changes, Kevin thought, but they keep reporting it.

"Awful," she said, facing him when the program moved to commercial. "This host is awful. Did you see how his eyes move left to right? You're not supposed to see that they're reading the teleprompter."

Behind them, in a cream-colored suede armchair, a patient was crying with high-pitched, newborn-like wails. And beside them, in an orange upholstered armchair, a patient sang a song that was toneless and rhythmic. Meanwhile, Sylvia remained lucid.

They used to call the Days Room the Dazed Room, which was altogether too easy a joke, but they made it anyway. The room was like a dozen living rooms smushed together, each with an armchair, a side table, a TV. Each with its own feel, its own style. There was an antique nook, a modern alcove, a rustic lodge. But there were no interior walls or doorways between them. It was all one space, an elevated platform to step up into with a perimeter of glass so the nurses could monitor everything happening inside.

Early on, Kevin had asked a nurse about this setup. He said, making light of it, "So did someone just forget about doorways, or . . . ?"

The nurse looked him up and down. "You ever walk into a room and forget why you went in there?" she said.

"Sure," Kevin said. "Is that bad?"

"No," said the nurse. "That's normal. You walked through a doorway. A door triggers a new scene in your brain. Walking through doorways makes people forget."

She was the tall nurse with the very short ponytail with frayed ends as if someone had cut a longer ponytail clean off. He watched her flit in and out of all the doorless rooms. Forgetting nothing, Kevin was certain, remembering everything.

She came, at last, to where they were watching what must have been an endless commercial break. She knelt in front of the armchair, blocking Kevin's view.

"Open up," she said to Sylvia. "Medicine time."

Kevin closed his eyes and pretended, for a second, to be far away from the doorless facility and standing instead inside his museum. He pictured all the doors in that building: the front door, the interior door to the lobby, the door on the locked electrical closet. He kept counting them. He imagined spending a night walking back and forth through all those doorways. In and out. Out and in. So that he could forget everything.

Sometimes he was jealous of Sylvia and how easily she let go of the past. He'd been trying all his life to hold on to it, to make sense of it. Why?

Her pills were swallowed and the nurse was gone and the TV was off. "I can't take any more of this garbage," she said. "Let's go for our walk."

She even knew they took walks together. It was such a good day.

Kevin helped her stand because he wanted to help her, but not because she needed the help. At lunch, the nurses sometimes asked Sylvia to open a jar for them. Physically, she had her strength, the same as ever. It was only her sense of the world that escaped her.

It had rained that morning, but the sun was back and the puddles and droplets were drying into the air so that the strong scent of grass was all around them. Three other pairs were taking slow walks and it struck Kevin that the patients looked just like the visitors. All elderly. He could just as easily be the one forgetting her.

Soon, there were more and more bad days. On those days, he reverted to his grumpiest, most persnickety self.

On a bad day, he flicked the TV on just to hear a voice because she herself had turned silent. He watched a sad report of a nearly dead girl. She had been lost in a fugue of time for over two decades, this girl. She was in a strange vegetative state. Her body didn't grow but she somehow still breathed.

He turned the volume up. There was the host's voice and a B-roll of footage:

"She sleeps in a bed at the center of the room. A silk headband is tied loosely into a bow at her forehead. Ringlets of hair fall off one shoulder. Her right arm rests above the blanket, palm up, as if asking for a hand to hold. She says nothing though her lips are slightly parted and, from time to time, her father will dab them dry of spit.

"She fell into this state after a near drowning at the age of eight. Doctors said she would stop breathing, but she did not stop breathing. Now, she is thirty-two and yet unaging. In all this time, only her hair and her nails have grown. Congregants once prayed to her on the front lawn and by her bedside. But for the last decade, she has not been seen."

Kevin was staring at the child on the television. "Do you remember me?" he whispered.

"Do you remember me?" Louder. "Do you know who I am?"

Sylvia turned in her armchair.

"Do you remember me?" Yelling now.

All the little rooms of the Days Room were quiet.

"Do you remember me?" Screaming it.

He felt his chest contract tightly as he kept asking. He had the sensation that he was in his museum, falling backward and backward through all human history, fast—as if weighed down by rocks—and then down and down, through a cave in the earth or through the heart of a whale.

25 Years of Sleep: The Case of the Jacob's Circle "Sleeping Child"

TIME LINE | TRANSCRIPT

HOST: As we approach the 25th anniversary of Maeve Wilhelm's near-drowning accident, *Time Line* is revisiting the strange case of the Jacob's Circle "sleeping child."

(INTRO MUSIC)

She sleeps in a bed at the center of the room. A silk headband is tied loosely into a bow at her forehead. Ringlets of hair fall off one shoulder. Her right arm rests above the blanket, palm up, as if asking for a hand to hold. She says nothing though her lips are slightly parted and, from time to time, her father will dab them dry of spit.

She fell into this state after a near drowning at the age of 8. Doctors said she would stop breathing, but she did not stop breathing. Now, she is 32 and yet unaging. In all this time, only her hair and her nails have grown. Congregants once prayed to her on the front lawn and by her bedside. But for the last decade, she has not been seen.

Every morning, the Congregants used to gather here, wearing orange robes. They would perform a long, complex ritual dance. It was a unique sight in this private, gated community of Jacob's Circle.

CONGREGANT: From the beginning, I think, the neighbors resented our presence.

When the Congregants raised funds to purchase the house across the street, they turned it into their chapel. Their numbers grew, and so did complaints.

The residents argued that the spectacle surrounding the girl amounted to nothing more than the exploitation of a helpless child. An official petition was passed around. Eventually, the community board put a stop to public worship.

NEIGHBOR: Jacob's Circle, we all agreed, it just isn't *zoned* for miracles.

(COMMERCIAL BREAK)

-17-

A QUARTER CENTURY OF SLEEP

DR. DEAN ADJUSTS THE CROSS OF HIS LEGS, WHICH ARE cramped in the crowded rows of uncomfortable seats.

He has been inside this museum only once, at a gala many years ago, which Genesix sponsored. That evening, he was busy mingling and networking and saw none of the exhibits, nor did he care to.

He takes in what he can see of the building's interior: the caves before him where the child is sleeping, the labyrinth of hallways to his left. It makes him tired, all this ancient history heaped into a fortress. He never cared for museums.

Behind this building: Grace Beach. He recalls the happiness he felt when he first saw the algae blooming. How he laughed because they'd done it here too, just as Naomi had predicted they could. It glistened red, the same way it had on Palmavja. A Lazarus species, that's what the scientists on Palmavja had called it. It had never gone extinct. Not fully.

The former Congregants sit in the front row and he studies them next—sad people in their ugly orange garments. Many of them have the same story: they had Prosyntus and they lost their memories and now they pray to an unaging, mostly dead girl. He can imagine the shame he is meant to feel when he thinks of it in those terms. But he cannot feel any real shame.

A lot of things are illegal.

Naomi said that to him and he has always remembered it because it was so close to a direct accusation. By then, he'd been floating above any implication for any wrongdoing for so long. That day, he had been jogging. She was with her daughter. He remembers all this. How she said that to him right in front of her child.

The litany is ending, finally: "Time is the accumulated pressure at a cluster of faults on a seafloor."

Dr. Dean does not join in the end of the recitation or the mumbled "Amen" that follows, but he does picture them—faults on a seafloor. This image makes him think of Palmavja again. Siegler's work on Palmavja was still underway when Dr. Dean started to sense that the whole elaborate project—the political kickbacks, the scapegoating of the indigenous youth, the aggressive and only semilegal sales tactics—could all unravel at any moment.

He was lucky to come across Naomi's research.

He made a bold proposition: he asked Siegler to close the foreign subsidiary and open a new domestic branch of one of his other companies, as close to Grace Beach as they legally could. Genesix was not even Siegler's most profitable enterprise. Dr. Dean was persuasive, sure, but it was her research that really convinced his boss.

From there, the company shifted focus and developed Prosyntus and no one spoke of Palmavja—or what they'd done there—again.

Years later, Dr. Dean watched Siegler's trial on TV. At the sentencing, he felt a sense of relief. Someone was being punished for the Palmavja crisis. And, even better, it wasn't him.

He heard his former boss say the word "guilty" thirty-five times, once for each charge. Hearing him say it, Dr. Dean wondered if there might be relief for Siegler too. After so long, an admission.

When Prosyntus failed, there was a class-action settlement. It was a financial loss, but Genesix recovered from it within the span of three years. The special agreement he arranged to use the waters off Grace Beach is still a secret; it is only his fear of this sleeping child that plagues him now.

What did the mother do to her?

He has a recurring dream about the girl. In it, she has a bluish complexion and her hair is so long—impossibly long—but as she sleeps, it grows longer still and then it begins to wind around his own body in tight, tight coils up his legs and his stomach and chest until he stops breathing.

The mother must have known *something*, he understands. So, had she tested it out on her daughter? An experiment with the algae? Was that what this was?

He kept close tabs on the sleeping child over the years.

He knew of the appearance of moths. He knew when they purchased the chapel—using money from the class-action settlement, in large part. He knew when the performance artist found her way to them. She was from Palmavja, he knew, originally. That unnerved him.

And then, for a time, the child was off-limits: closed to the public. He might have known the president of the Jacob's Circle Community Board. He might have helped make those quiet years quiet.

But now, after so long, she is back. They have moved her here to this museum. And this is exactly where Genesix and Kevin Marks made their arrangement.

Why *here*? he wonders. And again, he thinks of the mother. What did she know and who did she tell?

-18-

Twenty-four years into Maeve's sleep

LIONEL WAS IN THE KITCHEN DRINKING FRUIT PUNCH straight from the carton when he heard it: three knocks, repeated twice. Like a horse's gallop.

So much time had passed. And still, his hopes rose instantly. There she is, he thought. He left the fruit punch uncapped on the counter and went quickly to see her.

At the door, it was not his daughter. It was a man and a woman. Strangers.

"Hello," the man said. "I'm Mr. Marks."

"Marks?" Lionel echoed. "Francis Marks?" The name surfaced in his head from somewhere—the prize Naomi won. Wasn't it? The tangy punch was thick at the back of his throat. He coughed to clear it, but the sweetness would not ebb away completely.

"Francis was my father," Mr. Marks clarified. "And Francis Sr., my grandfather."

Lionel remembered now. "Right," he said, "famous men."

A nod.

He was struggling to adjust to this new fact, which was not a *new* fact at all. It was the same old fact he'd been living with for so many years: She was not here. He was alone.

"We're here for your daughter," Mr. Marks said. "We met her, years ago, at my museum."

"Your museum?" Lionel found he could not stop repeating whatever this man said as a question. But then . . . Marks, he thought again. Marks Museum. He was thinking of his daughter once more, and what she'd written in her letter. The Marks Museum of Human History. The doll of a boy who was sleeping there, those rocks.

She'd written to him nine years after she'd moved out. Another ten years had come and gone—eleven, twelve, thirteen years. Fourteen years now, almost fifteen. And though he wanted to write back to her, he could not do it. He hadn't heard from her again either. So that last thread of his family, he'd let slip away.

He'd read her letter over and over. But he hadn't tried to find any answers for her.

He hadn't *wanted* to find any answers. He thought of it this way: Once, he'd had a wife and two beautiful, identical daughters. But then came the ruptures. Naomi's death, Maeve's accident.

He had let the Congregants worship Maeve and he'd let the neighbors file their complaints about that worship. He hadn't tried to defend himself.

When the board had come to their decision, he had not appealed it. The chapel closed, the Congregants left. He had been alone—alone with Maeve—since.

Now, after all this time, two strangers had arrived on his doorstep from the Marks Museum, where that doll was. They'd used Evangeline's knock with the galloping rhythm. Maybe an answer would find *him*?

"I had a museum once," he offered.

"Oh?" said Mr. Marks. "History? Art?"

"Neither," Lionel answered. "Entomology. Bugs."

There was a finality to this pronouncement that he had not intended. An awkwardness settled.

"I'm Lionel." He extended a hand.

"This is Sylvia," the man said. "You can call me Kevin."

"Kevin?" Lionel said, echoing yet again. "My family knew a boat named *Kevin*." He could almost hear his girls giggling about that boat. "We really loved it."

KEVIN HAD NOT BEEN listening as the man spoke about boats and bugs. They'd taken seats in the kitchen, and Lionel poured coffee.

Kevin watched the milk disappear into his cup. What if he was wrong? What if, somehow, it was not her? He thought of preservation and what it was good for in a society that preserved only so that it could consume.

And of all those people—everyone who'd had Prosyntus—how they'd tried to preserve their bodies and ended up destroying their minds. All her Congregants.

And of his own childhood, growing up in the shadows of heroes who had become themselves names people might recognize vaguely as the father had, that was all.

Of Sylvia. He still loved her, despite the vacant expression she wore all the time. Very soon, the nurse said, she would lose her muscle memory: how to eat, how to speak, how to breathe eventually.

The human body was so horribly fleeting. And the glass case of memory, it just leaked and distorted the past it was meant to contain. This seemed to be the lesson the course of his life had been teaching him—until he found her.

He thought of the sleeping child, upstairs, breathing. The way she had looked on the news, unchanged after decades.

And it was her—right? A knot swam through his inner organs because what if it wasn't? But it was. Wasn't it? It had to be.

He had met her once. She had known him. The day when he'd first met Sylvia, it was that same field trip. He remembered. Her mother had died with red rocks in her pockets, and he had given the girl one of *his* rocks. So he was connected to her, this miraculous, unaging girl who had been preserved through all these years.

"Can we see her?" he blurted out. He might as well ask it outright. It was a long shot. He knew that no one had seen her in years.

"See her?" the father said. The father had been repeating everything Kevin said since they'd arrived. But now he paused, considering.

"All right," he said, "yes."

This seemed to surprise them all. They sat in silence for another second. Then rose.

SYLVIA HAD NOT BEEN in this house before. She did not think she had. In fact, she knew she had not. Had she?

For some reason, it felt familiar. This entire scene. And the front steps and the foyer and now this kitchen. She'd seen it somewhere. And the man—the father—had they met somewhere? No, she'd known a man like him. J. P.'s carpool: Evangeline's grandfather.

She was thinking about this in the kitchen and she was about to ask the father about that man and if they were maybe related, but he and Kevin stood and so she stood too and followed.

Where were they headed?

"You have a visitor," the father called at the doorway of a bedroom. Sylvia walked in first, and the father stayed behind at the door.

She approached the bed. She looked down at the girl. She saw it at once:

It was not her.

This girl who was sleeping looked different. She was younger than that girl from J. P.'s class had been. How could that be? Sylvia did not understand. But Sylvia did not understand lots of things. The girl was younger. She never knew where she was, really, in time. She leaned in, inspecting the child, just to be sure. She moved closer. And closer still. Inches from her. Closer. She stopped.

She breathed in. The girl breathed in.

She breathed out. The girl breathed out.

Another breath passed this way.

It must be peaceful, she thought, such a long, untroubled sleep.

But no, definitely, she saw, it was not Evangeline. It was someone who looked very much like her, a sister, or more likely a daughter. How much time had passed? A lot of time. Or no time at all.

"Sylvia—" said Kevin sharply.

"Please—" said the father.

She was leaning in very close to the girl. They didn't have to say more though because, already, Sylvia was standing up again.

On the way out, passing the father at the threshold, Sylvia turned. She said, very quietly so that Kevin did not hear, "She looks just like Evangeline."

The father's eyes widened. "You know her?" he whispered. "Evangeline?"

Yes! Sylvia thought, of course, yes, she had known Evangeline. J. P. had carpooled with her and Sylvia always liked the girl. Where had she gone? Did J. P. know? And where *was* J. P.? She missed him. She had so many questions, she always did, but she found—all at once—she could not ask them. She could not say anything.

For she had just forgotten how to speak.

KEVIN MARKS WAS NOT a great scientist or a famous explorer. There was no lasting contribution to history for which the name "Kevin Marks" would be known. He had been the owner of a mostly empty museum. He had spent his years in a massive building filled with aging relics and crumbling caves. When he died, he would not be remembered and neither would any of what he had tried to preserve.

He knew this.

But when he saw her, it no longer mattered.

The sleeping child.

She should have been in her thirties but she still appeared to be eight. She knew him, this girl. And he knew her. They'd had a connection. And here she was—breathing, sleeping, alive.

Kevin Marks was not greedy or religious. He did not expect any other miracle from her. He did not believe she was a symbol for anything, and he did not pray for her to wake up. It was enough to behold her as she was and would be. It was enough that she remembered to breathe, to sleep. That she didn't age.

It meant that she did remember.

It meant that she would go on remembering.

LIONEL STOOD STILL FOR several seconds. The woman had said his daughter's name and nothing afterward. Just the name and then she'd stopped speaking. The sound of the name hung in the air: *Evangeline. Evangeline. Evangeline.*

When he moved again, he felt as if he could return to an old way of life. The days when they'd dressed up for Halloween, when they'd played games in the snow, when they had been, for such a short time, a happy family. His hope reignited.

These two strangers, they did seem to be leading him to an answer now. And that answer might lead him back to Evangeline.

To an explanation he could give her. Of what had happened to her family and why.

Mr. Marks had been deeply moved by visiting Maeve. Lionel could see this. He began coming weekly with Sylvia to stand with her. That was all—just standing there. No dancing, no vows of silence, no fasting.

And then, Mr. Marks asked if he could plan an event for her. He'd like to invite the public.

The Congregants could not meet on the lawn to do their dance. They could not line up to see her. Lionel explained this. They could not watch her through the window. All of that had been banned. The community board had expressly prohibited all worship at Jacob's Circle.

But Mr. Marks had a different idea.

He wanted to mark the milestone they were approaching: a quarter century of sleep. They'd have to plan it all quickly—it was just a few months away—but he could do it, he said; he'd planned events like it before.

The thing was, he said, they'd have to move her.

"Move her?" Lionel said. "Where?"

Mr. Marks told him.

Now, Lionel was certain.

Fifteen years after Evangeline wrote him her letter, he sent her an invitation.

On the twenty-fifth anniversary of the accident, they would bring Maeve into the Caves of Adina inside the museum.

PART THREE

–19–

A QUARTER CENTURY OF SLEEP

SHE SLIPS IN LATE, RIGHT BEFORE THEY BEGIN RECIT-ing the litany. She takes a seat behind a pillar to the mezzanine, which hides her from her father at the front of the room.

To quiet her anxious mind, she thumbs the stone and pictures the objects that might be left in the caves: postcards, earrings, a wedding invitation. What else? Surely at least one obituary. Items even closer to garbage, probably: ticket stubs, receipts. Each of them a story that wants remembering.

It isn't fair. It's a childish thought but it's true. Why should her sister be the one to have to remember?

The museum owner walks to the podium. "Please rise," he says. He directs them to bring their offerings and form a line.

It is time to build the Archive of Sleep.

She makes her way forward. Nestled into the crowd, she can safely watch her father, who remains seated, observing without expression.

He's always been this way: silent, absent.

In that strange, lonely year after her sister's accident, he barely saw her. Even when he was looking at her, he was seeing her twin.

And after that year, he sent her off with her few belongings to live with a stranger and never spoke to her again. He didn't respond to her questions but it was never the lack of answers that hurt her. If she's being honest, it was how he might have joined her in at least *asking* them.

In any event, she doesn't need answers from him. She doesn't need anything from him anymore. She reminds herself of this as she takes her place at the end of the line and squeezes her stone.

SOMEBODY MUST KNOW SOMETHING.

After she got the invitation and discovered the photograph from the gala, this was all she kept thinking. Every morning, she woke up planning to book her flight and purchase a ticket to the ceremony, but she couldn't let herself go through with it.

"Somebody must know something." She'd say it aloud to try to convince herself that she needed to go there and find out.

Two weeks went by like this. One evening, she dug out the leather pouch where she kept the red, shimmering rock—the one the museum owner had given her as a child. She poured the rock out into her hand and held it to the light, watching it gleam.

"Somebody must know something," she said.

She remembered all the questions she'd had about these rocks, all the questions she'd been unable to answer.

The red orb looked like Mars, and the thought of Mars reminded her of a woman she'd known once, a lifetime ago, who had read to her from a list about space.

The woman had been visibly sick. She'd had a big, bald head and long, skinny fingers. They'd sat on a bench together and the woman had shown her a notebook of lists.

She hadn't thought of this woman in what felt like eons. She'd nearly forgotten her, but now she remembered all of this: riding her bike to the cemetery to visit her mother's grave, taking grave rubbings of the headstone. This was when she was still living at her childhood home, still learning to live a life twinless.

All this time, and her sister had had neither a grave nor a headstone.

It wasn't fair.

The scrapes on her arm were scabbing, healing already. She rubbed the rock against them.

If you keep scratching for answers, it scars. Her grandfather's old advice.

Somebody might know something, but whatever it was, it wouldn't matter any longer.

She put the rock back in the leather pouch, the leather pouch back in the drawer.

"I'll see you Friday for dinner," she told her grandfather. She had booked the trip finally. This was a week ago. "I'll stay the night, and on Saturday, I'll go to the ceremony at the museum."

"You decided to go," he said with a tinge of surprise.

"I decided to go," she repeated.

She did not need to go to seek any answers, but, she knew, she needed to go.

ONE BY ONE, SHE sees people disappear into the caves. They reappear after a moment, looking bereft, with tears in their eyes.

She feels flushed, sweaty. The stone is pleasantly cool against her hand.

What does the archive contain by now? An unsent love note? A popsicle stick with a joke on it? A lock of hair? A foreign coin?

Her fist clenches, unclenches.

She moves forward, turning away from her father. She feels certain that he won't recognize her and she does not want to give him the chance to prove her correct.

It's her turn.

She shuts her eyes as she steps into the Caves of Adina so that they can adjust to the darkness. She takes the stone out before she opens her eyes again.

The rock is not red, and it does not sparkle.

She let them go, truly, all the questions she had about those rocks. Instead, she brought this stone—it is gray, dull. They found it together. She and her sister, one Saturday with their mother on one of their digs.

"It's a perfect heart!" her sister called, gleeful.

"Let me see!" she demanded, grabbing it.

It was true: a perfect heart.

"Can we keep it?" they begged their mother.

Their mother inspected it. "You know, this isn't what a human heart looks like," she said. But she let them keep it regardless.

They were so excited. The stone was sandy, and they rinsed it with their bottle of water and dried it on a towel gently. They traded off holding it as they walked back up the hill home.

They kept it in the jar that held their sea glass collection.

She brought it with her when she moved to her grandfather's house, and for a quarter century, she's carried it with her.

And this is something that nobody knows any longer.

Not the Congregants, who never met her sister but who expected that her sister would somehow remember them.

Not the neighbors, who knew her sister only as an inconvenience in the neighborhood.

Not even her father, though he knew it once. If she is angry at him, it is because he's forgotten this small and very obvious fact:

That she was a *child* before she was the sleeping child.

Evangeline looks at Maeve.

Maeve's face is the way her own face used to be. Peaceful. Asleep. She feels old, tired, but resolute as she stares at her sister. She kisses the heart-shaped stone and opens Maeve's palm.

Maeve had a life, she thinks. But what life she had ended a long time ago. It isn't fair that her sister should have to go on only to serve as a vessel for everyone else's memories.

She moves Maeve's finger to touch the one sharp corner of the heart, and she says goodbye to her sister.

SEVERAL THINGS HAPPEN AT the same time all the time.

One might call this a "simultaneity" or a "coincidence." It doesn't necessarily imply any sort of grand plan.

For instance, on the ocean floor, a seismic shift can occur just as a thirty-three-year-old woman touches her sister's finger to the sharp point of a stone.

And as scenes from childhood flood back to her: a made-up game where they hopped atop a layer of snow; their mother blowing a kiss by the front door; their father dressed in a cow suit.

And as she hears a low rumble.

Quiet at first but getting louder.

"Run," she can say in her very next breath.

IN THE CENTRAL HALL, the ground is buzzing.

"Run," a voice says from the caves, but no one can hear it.

There is the noise of rock falling. It starts like this: quick, quick, long. Lionel startles as if he's awoken, and a woman rushes from the caves toward the podium. She leans forward and grabs the microphone.

"Run," she says again. "Everyone, run."

Now, they are rushing to the exit.

They are running haphazardly. They are forming a mass and pushing toward the doors, where they are stepping on each other's toes.

Sylvia is imagining J. P. as a baby because she is swept up by a man—Luke—who carries her infant-like through the throng.

Monique has a flash of reminiscence too: fleeing with her sisters through a vacant lot and into a doorless vehicle.

The earth moves in violent waves that Dr. Dean imagines are the punishment he's avoided for so long. He fears it will swallow him.

Together they sway and they list and they keel.

EVANGELINE KNEW THE CAVES would collapse. She doesn't know how she knew. But she knew. So somebody did know something, she thinks.

The ground is slowing back to stillness. The foundation of the museum is cracked, the roof sunken. On the shoreline, the crowd huddles. Safe. She was able to save them. All of them.

Almost all of them.

In the mad flight out of the building, her father pushed and pushed against the current, trying to go in the opposite direction.

"Excuse me, excuse me," he kept saying, rather buffoonishly.

She paused there for one fraction of one second. Enough time to witness it.

Is it a miracle?

She asks herself this as she walks toward the ocean, propelled by a calm, acceptant kind of solitude.

She came to say goodbye to her sister and now—at long, long last—her sister is gone.

So is it a miracle?

Her father entered the caves and then the caves collapsed, burying him with his daughter. He acted fast, and what's more—he *acted*. For once in his life, he rose to the occasion. She is grateful. That he was with her sister, in the end. That she has this final memory. And yes, she would say, it's a miracle.

She will turn and leave in another few minutes, but first, she wants to watch the waves tower and break unpredictably. The sky is a hazy yellow. There is no rain, no wind. The sea sprays her face and runs down her cheeks, chest, arms, and there are no people around her.

It feels like the moment right after the world ends.

But—what is *that*?

A dark shadow bobs at the water's rough surface.

Her mother? she thinks, strangely. Of course not, no.

It is a man.

–20–

Twenty-five thousand years before Maeve's sleep

BOTH KNEES HURT, MY HIP HURTS, AND MY FINGERS hurt at the first knuckle. The pain has two distinct registers. There is the dull, broad pulse all around the joints, and there is the high-pitched screech at the center: thin, sharp. It ebbs and flows but does not disappear completely.

What else is like that pain? they asked me.

Nothing, I answered.

But I might have said: *Memory. Time.*

If not for my children, I would have died long ago—starved to death or eaten by some other starved animal. I used to dream up ways I could repay them, but I did not think I would ever be able to, and then the Disappearance came.

The Disappearance changed many things but not everything.

I still have my children, who are grown, though all the young children are gone. My children still care for me. *Pa*, they call me. Sometimes, *Papa*.

My sons do not rush through the tasks of my care, but they arrive two at a time to split up the work. They go about it with an efficiency that I do not like to disrupt: making a balm from the red sea plant to rub on my joints, gathering seeds, making bundles of herbs to ward off pests. They do not linger.

Sleep well, they say, already walking away from me.

When she is able, my daughter comes in the evenings.

Last night, she held a hand out, letting me squeeze it as the pain in my knees was at its worst.

Once I could let go and breathe again, she pushed the hair from my temples and let the breeze cool me. I remembered doing the same for her when she was a fussy baby: patting her head, waiting for sleep.

When I looked up at her round face and crooked smile, I almost told her everything. But then I thought: She doesn't feel pain, but I can still hurt her.

What is it? she asked, seeing that I had moved to speak.

Thank you, I said instead, closing my eyes.

Once, there were children.

This is a story I tell them.

The children filled the island with noises. There was the sweetness of their laughter, the animal sound of their cries.

When the children were gone, I say, *they were gone completely. There were no clues or traces to follow. No footprints, no clothing, no scent.*

Were the children in the caves? they asked, early on.

I answered this truthfully. *No.*

Our caves are said to connect us, in death, to our lost twin ancestors.

They forget this story too, so I tell them.

It is said that our island's first people swam from another island that was identical to our own. It was a long swim and the red sea plant is said to have been a parting gift. Waking up to see these first swimmers leaving, the others put handfuls of red flowers in the waves and the flowers followed them across the water.

I cannot control when a memory presents itself. I have tried to explain this, but they do not even *remember* remembering.

Is it like dreaming? my daughter asked.

If anything, it is the opposite of dreaming. It is like waking up when you thought you were already awake. But I did not want to embarrass her for asking the question.

Yes, I said, *it is like dreaming.*

MY DAUGHTER'S SON WAS the first boy born to his generation. We loved him and called him our prince. He was lean with deep brown eyes and scabs on his elbows. There was a muskiness we never could rinse from his hair.

When he fainted, I was the one who saw him. I ran, frantic, into the water. I remember the denseness of his body, the noise of his breath.

I do not remember everything. How I managed to run or to carry him in my state. But I remember the piercing in my shoulder as I lifted him. I was feeling this same sensation in the same part of my body when the whole scene came back to me.

For this reason, I am thankful for the pain. Without it, the recollection and the boy himself would be lost.

The boy's father sits close to me when I tell my stories. I can smell his hair, which has a similar scent. His eyes look just like the boy's eyes.

I tell them what I remember, but I remember more than I tell.

BEFORE THE DISAPPEARANCE, I was a useless person they kept alive. Now I have a reason to go on living: I protect them from what they do not remember.

When the children were gone, there were long days and nights filled with pain.

This is not a story. It's true.

No one came to me with a soothing balm or to carry me out of the sun. Pain was everywhere. It was an eerie loneliness. To share what had once been mine.

The island was quiet. There were only the waves and the howling beasts and the rolls of distant thunder. Everyone was grieving what had happened to the children, which—at that point—they knew.

They were never, in reality, *gone*; the children had fallen into an unwakeable sleep.

As they slept, I hardly moved. It became too painful. My bones stiffened like rock. My fingers gnarled like roots. I found an arrowhead, and with halting movements, I sliced the skin on the back of a leg so that I could watch my own blood and see, for a time, where the pain was coming from.

I pictured jumping off the high hill. Leaping into the rocks. I could neither walk to the high hill nor jump. Still, I kept picturing it.

It was the rainy season, and as often happened, crawling bugs gathered where I slept. I could not pick them off or move to kill them.

One evening I saw that the bugs too were gone, having cocooned themselves in threads that hung below my last bundle of herbs.

I was alone.

I fed myself sand in huge handfuls, hoping this might kill me. It did not kill me. It only left me thirsting terribly.

I was unable to reach any water, unable to die. But with a strength that did not belong to me, I finally managed to grab the pitcher.

I fell to the ground holding it, and at that same moment the cocoons burst open.

Dozens of winged creatures flocked out. Their wings brushed against my cheeks as they circled. I could see nothing but that flickering. I had never seen anything like it and I laughed, despite everything.

That is how I learned that the pain would not kill me.

To seek shade, I could get on all fours and drag my lower body across the ground with my forearms. My skin would scrape and bleed, but that would barely register against the screaming in my joints, and yet I would get to the wide-leafed tree on my own.

I gathered seeds, biting on my tongue through the cramping in my fingers. Once, I bit right through the tip of my tongue. As I fed myself, I swallowed both seeds and blood. Nonetheless, I learned I could feed myself.

The children kept sleeping; the island grieved; time kept passing, but it was like no time passed at all. It was a single, interminable night of nights refusing to break into a new day.

I do not know who first discovered the sea plant's miraculous abilities. I was alone with my pain when it happened.

I watched them begin to take bowls of the plant into the caves.

These caves were part of our most sacred ritual. We entered them only to lay down our dead. Inside, we drummed and danced, and the echoes were said to carry the spirit all the way over to our lost twins.

What were they doing with those bowls of the red plant? I kept watching.

More people came, and more, until it seemed everyone on the island—except for me and the sleeping children—had gone into the caves.

I thought about joining them. It would be a painful climb but I knew I could do it.

Still, someone should stay with the children.

They may have left me behind for that reason.

I do not know what they did inside the caves. I could feel the vibrations and I imagined them dancing wildly to the drumbeat we reserved for the dead. Perhaps they were killing themselves, I thought sadly.

Finally, exhaustion must have claimed them. All sound ceased.

When they climbed out of the caves the next morning, it was done; they had rid themselves of the past.

They no longer remember.

How the children watched the fire in awe. Or how they'd compete to collect the most stones from the beach. How their teeth loosened and fell out. Or the monotony of repeating the same warnings to them. *Don't!* And: *Careful!* And: *Stop!*

A vague sorrow remains, but it is as if they have walked around with it all their lives.

People can grow used to anything, I think when I speak to them.

The sea plant took more than their memories from them.

They have stopped aging. Wrinkles do not unwrinkle, but they do not become any deeper. And pain: things that I would expect to hurt them no longer do. Stepping on a sharp shell with a bare foot or exposing the skin to the sun.

They suffer only painless consequences.

They vomit without any sense that they are going to vomit.

They do not know they are bleeding until they see their own blood. Their bodies are sources of wonder in this way.

Moons and moons and moons have passed and life has gone on. Also, it has shortened. Since drinking the plant, my people die young.

They do not seem to regret it. They know—because I've told them—how grief cast a silence over the island.

The days must feel better now, louder, lighter. It must not matter that there are fewer of those days or that, without any warning, those days will end.

Through all of this, they left me behind. It was a choice that I made too—not going to the caves to join them. I do not regret my choice either.

I alone will remember, just as I alone will grow old and I alone will feel pain.

Pain, age, and memory have come to feel the same to me.

AFTER I PULLED OUR prince from the ocean, I collapsed in a heap on the shore.

Pa? I heard voices call from somewhere. *Pa! Papa!*

When my eyes opened, the boy's father was standing above me.

What have you done? he yelled. *What did you do?*

The sea plant was rolling in with the waves, catching around me, thicker than I'd ever seen it.

He forced me to my feet and held my arms behind my back and pushed me along. I kept tripping. My daughter came up behind, trailing us, carrying the boy, who—unbelievably—remained sleeping. I remember seeing, in the distance, figures by the caves. A gathering. Why was everyone standing there? What were they waiting for? Who had died?

My knees screamed. I could hear my daughter humming to the boy and I pretended she was humming to me. This helped me keep moving and not cry out and shame myself.

At the mouth of the cave, I was thrust forward.

My son, the man said. But before he could tell them whatever he believed I had done to the boy, other voices spoke.

Yes, all of our children, they said. *They have fallen asleep.*

WE DID NOT KNOW how to care for the sleeping children. Their lips cracked like dry soil. Their skin paled. They breathed but ate nothing, drank nothing.

There was no complete disappearance. There was this slow fading. Alone with the children, I watched them slip from sleep into death.

While everyone else was in the caves, I began digging. I dug on the far west of the island, near to the shore.

However long I live, I do not think I will know a worse agony than I felt those days when I stayed aboveground, digging holes for the sleeping bodies of my children's children, so I will not try to put words to it.

My daughter's son was the last child I buried.

His fingernails had grown long, as had his hair. I touched his ears and his round face and I laid him down in that hole I had dug for him, slightly farther away from where the other children lay.

I spent that night creating a doll of the boy because I did not want to let him go completely. It hurt my hands to carve, but I ignored the pain until I was finished. I made it so that his eyes were closed and I put the doll in a gesture of sleep. I pressed the red rocks into his gown to make him glow and I gave him a crown.

When I was finished, I spoke to him.

One day, I said out loud to the prince, *people will know your story.*

I did not intend to lie to him. I did not know that I would be the only one who would hold on to his memory. But I like to think that it was not a lie. It was another story I was telling.

Sleep well, I said.

Good night, Pa, I imagined him answering as, painfully, I covered his body with earth.

–21–

Eleven months into Maeve's sleep

July

A WOMAN AND A girl are walking the winding paths of a cemetery's rolling green hills when the woman says she wants to stop to sit and maybe stretch for a minute. The truth is, she feels dizzy.

They find a bench and stand beside it, debating whether it is the same bench where they sat when they first met a few months ago. They like to try to sit on that same bench, but more and more often, they are uncertain. All the benches look the same.

The woman is contemplating the bench as she might a work of art while also biding time to catch her breath and stop the world from spinning.

Eventually, the girl runs out of patience. She says, decisively, "If we agree it's the same bench, then it's the same bench."

The woman teases, "What are you, an epistemologist?"

And the girl says nothing, but she gives the woman a bemused expression. They sit.

When she feels better, the woman flips through her notebook. "How about 'Astounding Animal Facts'?" she offers.

"Are the animals astounding," the girl asks, "or the facts?"

"What are you," the woman asks, "a copy editor?" She doesn't wait for an answer. She starts reading.

This will be the last list they ever read together.

May

THERE WERE THREE KINDS of things, Evangeline thought while biking to the cemetery for the very first time: living, non-living, and dead.

She wasn't allowed to bike as far as the cemetery or stay out as late as sunset, but she rode her bike a little farther and stayed out a little later anyway because, why not? There was nothing else to do and no one to do it with. And besides, no one would notice.

Her sister was not fully dead. That was what all the machines in the bedroom with their constant beeping were about. But Evangeline had learned that the borders between the three kinds of things were not as set as most people might like. There were gray areas. Her sister seemed much more dead than she was living, and maybe more nonliving than dead?

She biked hard and fast, pedaling even when she might have stopped pedaling to coast for the downhill portions. This warmed her body, which was already warm from the late spring heat, and sweat gathered under her blue hat. When she arrived, she ditched her bike near the cemetery's arched gate and ran down into a gully. She lay there.

Was her mother level with her now, or still deeper?

That was when she heard crying.

"Hello?" Evangeline called. "Hello? Who's there?"

The crying stopped. A woman approached the edge of the gully, peered down.

"Hello," they called to each other at the same instant. The woman did not look like she had been crying. She looked sick. Her head was completely hairless and her skin had a reddish tinge.

"I'm climbing out," Evangeline said. "Wait."

She imagined the scene from the woman's eyes. While crying, you find a child inside a ditch in a cemetery. You watch her climb up out of it. Could the woman think she was a ghost who had gotten lost crawling out of a grave? It seemed possible.

She didn't want to scare the woman. But she didn't mind seeming like a ghost either. It made sense that she would be one. She was invisible a lot of the time already.

She crawled out of the ditch and went to the woman. She saw that the woman was taller than she was, obviously, but not by so much. Shorter than her mother. And how old? Evangeline used to believe age came in two categories: you were either young or old. But she had come to see that this was not an even way to divide things. "Young" was only a sliver, which "old" far outweighed. Once you got old, you were old forever.

Could you even remember what it felt like to be young once you crossed over? She doubted it.

The woman looked old enough to be a mother but younger than her own mother was. Was or is? It didn't matter. When you died, you stopped getting older.

THE BENCH THEY SAT on was not far from the cemetery entrance and an empty row of what would become plots. One would be Tess's grave in the future. Not the distant future either.

Tess held her notebook out on her lap, hands folded on its worn-edged yellow pages. The girl had scooted all the way forward so that her short legs could bend comfortably over the seat edge. Even still, her feet hung inches above the earth.

The girl was staring at Tess's fingers and Tess was watching her stare at them. She was aware of how they must look. They had thinned to mere bones that bulbed out at the nail beds. She was not embarrassed, but she wanted to distract them both from those fingers for a minute.

"Want to see my lists?" Tess asked.

She opened her notebook and thumbed through to show the girl. There was her list of two-word names for fireworks (these were her inventions: "dirty loofah," "mutated urchin," "shoulda-beena dud"). Next, her list of restaurants where the entrées were numbered, making the menus themselves into lists (she had been ordering in order at each of them: her first visit, the number one; her second, the number two; and so on). Back to the cover, which she had made into a table of contents, so it functioned also as the first list. She had titled it grandly: "List of Lists Contained Herein."

Tess passed the girl the book and let her comb through it. She could tell the girl was impressed. Children were funny. How old was the girl? Eight?

She might know basic math, Tess imagined. And she might love stories, but she was at an age where she could still struggle with reading. That was a frustration she remembered. There on the bench, she recalled what learning to read had felt like.

At first, it was a new world to explore. But then, no. It hadn't been close enough. Tess remembered this part and could still feel the sting of it. She could see that world but she couldn't get there, not yet. She'd had to practice and it got harder and harder and she'd learned then how there would never be enough of it: time. This was something she was still learning, somehow.

She supposed being at the end of life made you remember the beginning better.

She pitied the girl next to her, who must have been going through this all now.

Or not? The girl could be a terrific reader. She might not need Tess's pity at all. Tess didn't know the girl. She was just sitting with her in a cemetery on a bench, trying to feel sad for someone else to stave the self-pity she'd been drowning in moments before.

The girl's bike lay next to the gate, toppled onto its side for lack of a kickstand. She wore a blue hat but no helmet. And here she was, alone and talking to a perfect stranger at dusk in a cemetery. All of this told Tess some things about the girl that she felt she *did* know with a high degree of certainty. The girl's loneliness, she could see it. And so, she pitied the girl again and some more.

EVANGELINE TRIED TO THINK of other things that were like ghosts. She had liked seeing the woman's lists and was thinking she could start her own. Her parents had both been scientists—her father still was. Once, her father had said that a scientist loves a good taxonomy. She had asked what a taxonomy was and had not felt ashamed to ask her own father what a word meant.

Okay, she thought, so "Things That Are Like Ghosts."

What else was like a ghost?

She'd attended a birthday party the day before at a roller rink. When the party was over, her father hadn't shown up to get her, not after what felt like two hours of waiting. The birthday boy and his father had driven her home in their own car.

The boy's father had said "I'm sure everything's fine" at least four times on the short ride, and the way he looked at her in the mirror made her know that he was sure everything was not fine. She had felt that she might punch the birthday boy who'd just had such a great party and was still smiling stupidly while, a few inches away from his face, something horrible was happening to her, again. She had sat on her hands to stop herself in case the urge overcame her.

When they got to her house, she unbuckled and ran out before the car was parked and knocked three times—quick, quick, long—before thrusting the door open herself.

Inside, everything was just as it ought to be.

Her father sat at the table, observing his ants, taking notes. "Oh," he said. His head bounced up. "There you are."

"Here I am," Evangeline said.

She watched as her father turned his attention back to his ants. Down the hall, she heard the beeps of machines. It was all just the same, she thought, when she was there and when she was not there.

She wondered about her next birthday. Where would she have her party? Inside the supermarket? Why not? Her father had left her there twice in two months. She knew each numbered aisle now and what it contained. Very suddenly, she wanted to cry, thinking of her next birthday and dreading it with her twin sister asleep in that bed.

She could think of nothing else that was very much like a ghost.

The oldest gravestones in the distance were thin and crooked. How about that? What else was shaped like the gravestones? She could start her lists there. "Objects Shaped Like Gravestones."

She thought: Teeth in a witch's mouth. That was a spooky thing to say in a cemetery, so she said it.

"Those graves look like teeth in a witch's mouth," she said.

"They do," the woman said.

But Evangeline was stuck once more because—what else?

Above them, the sky was darkening, and Evangeline thought about everything she could not see from the bench.

Space. Should she make a list for that?

"What's it like in space?" she asked the woman. She wasn't yet good at this list stuff. She figured she could use some help.

The woman looked at her strangely. She closed her eyes. Opened them. Glanced upward. Then she flipped to a page in her notebook: "What It's Like in Space," the woman said and cleared her throat.

She could tell the woman was fake-reading. None of what she said next was written down.

"WHAT'S IT LIKE IN space?" the girl asked.

Tess tried to see herself as the girl must see her. There were her alien hands. The orb of her head, which was totally hairless. And her complexion, a red that was not ruddy with health but more like irritated all over, as if from the inside out. Her skin had become a surface much like a terrestrial planet's; it was fretted and scalloped on her neck, collapsed and cratered on her forehead, eroded and cliffed at the back of her head. She could make a list for it. "Topography of My Skin."

Was it possible, Tess wondered, that the girl thought she was a Martian?

The lists, too, those might seem—to the girl—like further evidence. Observations a visitor would make on a new world.

The girl was waiting for her to answer. Tess breathed as if preparing to speak but then looked up at the moonless sky. What else was out there?

Anything?

On the bench, she met the girl's gaze squarely. Her eyes were serious, Tess saw, older than the rest of her somehow.

If the girl saw Tess as a Martian, she'd be a Martian.

"Let's see," Tess said. She flipped to a page and pretended to read from it, holding it close to her chest so that the girl, if she could read, would not be able to read what it said.

EVANGELINE ALREADY KNEW THAT, in a way, they were in it now. Everyone. That they were always in it, space, moving in a stretched-out circle on a sphere that itself spun in a circle and on a tilt. She knew that the galaxy, also, was spinning and that it was spinning around a black hole. And that a black hole was not empty but the exact opposite, which was why it seemed like it really was empty.

Sometimes identical things were very different.

Sometimes opposite things were alike.

Her father had wanted to be a space scientist when he was young, but now he was old and he studied bugs. He had told her many facts about space that she had not understood. Like the strength of a gamma-ray burst and the kinds of light that could not be seen by human eyes. What about ghost eyes? she wondered. Could they see it? She stared up at nothing.

Or maybe she had understood these things, all of them; she just couldn't imagine them. You could know something was true without feeling the truth of it.

Like, was her sister *really* alive still?

And like, would her mother *always* be dead? Yes. But she could not believe it. She could start a list for that: "Truths That Do Not Feel True."

There were many things she would list there. That was a good list to start with, finally. Like, how the enormous size of space meant humans could not be alone in it. This was something her father loved to talk about. You could know this and still feel, inside your own body, a different truth, which was that you were alone.

And what about being a ghost? She was not a ghost, she knew, even if she felt like one. Although—did ghosts know they were ghosts?

"Do ghosts know they're ghosts?" Evangeline asked, momentarily brave. She said it only half like a question and she wanted to take it back as soon as it was out.

"Never mind," she said hurriedly. "Don't answer that. Go on."

TESS KEPT FAKE-READING FROM a list of space that was not in her notebook. Of its silence: so thick it could funnel into your ears and fill up your head with a new brain of white noise.

And of the color of Mars: how it was red from the same compound found in blood.

And of the darkness—a paradox because it should be bright with the light of a billion, trillion stars.

She pretended to read of where that darkness came from, which might be from the growing distance of stars that were moving—all the time—away from you, like an ambulance siren shifting in pitch from high to low, as it left you behind.

And she pretended to read of the vacuum: what air felt like when it had no temperature, when it wasn't "air" either, and how the complete lack of pressure meant your body, if your body were out there, would vaporize as the water inside it spread out and out and out until it was lost.

She paused, having heard herself. She'd been speaking of space like a kind of death. She hadn't meant to. And the girl was a worrier, Tess thought, seeing how her brow kept furrowing while the rest of her face was unchanged

She added, "But it's beautiful too. So beautiful. I can't even explain it. Don't worry."

"I'm not worried," the girl said.

June

EVANGELINE DECIDED TO GO early to the cemetery, before the woman would be there. She wanted to take a grave rubbing.

She didn't really like the way the grave rubbing came out, but it was okay. She could make another one some other time. That grave would be there.

When she finished, she looked up, and there was the woman across the hill. She didn't get it, did the woman live in the cemetery? Every Sunday, she was already there before Evangeline arrived.

Earlier that week, Evangeline had been left at the supermarket yet again. Her father still called her by her sister's name just as much as her own. And at the string of recent birthday parties, she had been the very last one picked up from the roller rink and the bowling alley and the arcade. She'd heard the sound of tape ripped off balloons over and over.

Was there anything worse, she thought, than waiting with another kid's parents for yours to arrive?

Of course there was. How could she think that? Her sister wasn't anywhere with anyone waiting for anything, and that must be the worst kind of boredom there was.

She thought of those elderly people breathing their stale breath over her sister, praying silently. What were they praying for? What did they think her sister could *do*?

The woman was waving. She waved back. The woman can see me, Evangeline thought. But that doesn't mean I'm not a ghost.

They sat on a bench, and the woman let Evangeline see her notebook again. The cemetery gate creaked in the wind. It wasn't a scary noise. It was a funny imitation of a scary noise. Evangeline almost laughed at it.

She had thought she'd be scared, alone in a cemetery, but nothing ever scared her here. What could scare a ghost? Anything?

Evangeline skimmed through the lists, wanting to read all of them from beginning to end, but there wouldn't be time for that. Already, she saw, the sun was setting.

She flipped through faster. She saw the list of movies with snakes in them and the list of astounding animal facts and the list of news headlines. She should pick one, she realized. One list to read all the way through. So she turned to a page at random.

"Objects Shaped Like My Fingers," she read to herself.

She had seen the woman's hands. The fingers were skinny bones that bloomed out at the tips.

She read: "Flower pistils."

She read: "Stirring spoons."

She read: "Marks Island," which she knew was not an actual island but a blob with a very narrow bridge of land attached to it.

She read: "Lollipops."

There was one more item on the list. It was "Sperm."

She read: "Sperm" and did not know what sperm was so she turned to the cover quickly, closing the book and giving it back to the woman. It was a childish feeling and she hated it. That particular humiliation when you had to admit that you did not know a word.

At the birthdays, while the other kids were getting picked up by their parents, Evangeline watched tired teens in baggy sweat-shirts peel crepe paper off beige walls. She thought how similar these places all were, underneath.

Evangeline had already forgotten some birthday parties she'd gone to, and it made her half-happy, half-sad to know that some of what was happening now she would later forget.

The deflating balloons had looked like the woman's fingers, though.

"Deflating balloons," she said, to hear her own voice more than anything.

And the woman knew at once why she had said it and she liked it so she wrote it down on the list.

WHEN TESS SAW THE girl that day, she was halfway down the path, holding a supersized crayon and a piece of paper. She did not know what the girl was doing. It was June, and they had met like this already a few times. Tess knew by then that the girl was odd. When the girl saw her, Tess waved. She saw the girl fold the paper and tuck it into a front pocket of her shorts. They met in the middle.

The paper made a crinkling sound every other step, reminding Tess of something. Dry leaves? There were no dry leaves here, only burnt grass. Summer had not officially started but already the sun was blistering and the earth, scorched. She ran a hand over her own bald head and felt its nakedness.

"Deflating balloons," the girl said after they had found what they thought was their bench.

"Good one," Tess said. She took the notepad, leaned it against her left forearm to write. Under the list called "Objects Shaped Like My Fingers," she added a bullet and two words: "Deflating balloons."

Tess looked at her fingers while writing. They *did* look like deflating balloons.

The longer she looked, the more she felt they were unattached to her. Alien fingers, she thought. Martian hands. It was a weird sensation. She wiggled them out in front of her body, turned her palms up and down.

She read "Deflating balloons" there in its fresh ink and tried to stop reading it and instead stare at the letters so they would not look like letters anymore but mere shapes. Once you knew how to read a language, you could not unknow it. The letters kept on being letters and the words kept on being words.

She rubbed a phantom finger across the new entry, smudging it as if to erase it. But it was written in pen, so the ink only spread.

In the hospital, there had been a bouquet of balloons beside her bed when she woke up. It was the first thing she had seen after surgery.

The balloons were bright and shiny, inflated and dumb.

"Get well!" one read, like a command.

Don't tell me what to do, she thought. The way Tess remembered it, she had known, in the instant of waking, that the surgery had not been a success. This awareness had dawned and she'd seen a future, which was her future and her future alone.

She had punched a balloon with as much strength as she could muster, which was not very much strength at all. It made a soft crinkling that woke her husband, who had been sleeping in the recliner beside the bed.

"You're up," he said, hopeful.

She swallowed. She had a dry, bitter taste in her mouth. It might have been a new taste she had for this life, for this world.

She tried to mask it.

"Yes," she said.

"How do you feel?" he asked.

She could not turn to face him. Why should she have to find a silver lining for him in everything? A balloon finished a half rotation and the fluorescent light bounced off its shimmering backside, taunting her. Tears came to her eyes but her husband could not see them and she did not let them fall.

She was lying away from him when she said in a whisper of a sarcastic singsong, "I'm good. How are you?"

Tess had real lists about space now, with facts she'd corroborated through her own research. Not just stuff she improvised on the spot as she had the first time when the girl had asked her what space was like.

There was a list of what her weight would be on other planets and planetoids. A list of the lengths of their days and their years. A list of star names and classifications. A list of distances in terms of other distances; everything was relative in space, she had learned. You always had to pick a reference point. How many school bus lengths equal one light-year? How many kilograms of dynamite equal the sun?

There was nothing inherently bleak about these lists. Still, they did not feel, exactly, cheerful. Was anything cheerful in space? It seemed not.

She was reading these to the girl and she was feeling, for once, a lack of pressure. There was no need in this cemetery, on this bench, to be anything—entertaining, optimistic. She could just be a Martian now, if that was what the girl thought she was. That was nice.

The girl's head caught her attention. It was different. She had a double whorl, Tess saw. She'd never seen it before. The blue hat the girl had worn until then had covered it.

"Where's your hat?" Tess asked, interrupting herself.

The girl told the story of the hat's disappearance. It was a sad story and it reminded Tess of how her husband talked of negative space. Negative space—the emptiness around the subject in an image. Her husband was a photographer, an almost obsolete hobby. He had a room in their apartment filled with portraits of her. Just that. It was separate from the room he used as his darkroom. This was a room where, piled up in corners and laid out across all the surfaces, there were images of her own body and face.

Sometimes, she would go into that room to be surrounded by herself. She found it meditative, a transcendental experience. She could turn off her brain and body and be there in a room with other, former versions of her brain and body captured and printed in two dimensions.

Some photos were posed. Many were candid. Most she did not feel were really of her. She knew they *were* her, but she could not feel the truth of that.

But it was the space around her in the photographs, that was what she'd try to focus on. Everything that was not her and would go on without her.

All space is negative space once the subject is gone.

"WHERE'S YOUR HAT?" THE woman asked.

Evangeline still felt the presence of the blue hat there where it should have been. It was windy and her hair blew all over. The woman's own head was totally bald. Did she ever have hair? If so, how did she lose it?

There were questions they never asked each other.

Above them, the trees were green and flowering. She thought of how, once autumn came, the leaves would dry up and fall and be buried in snow and how, when the snow melted, all the leaves would be gone.

Evangeline very much disliked to misplace things, but she often misplaced things. Small things, usually. A puzzle piece, a pair of scissors, a heart-shaped stone that was lost for a day before she found it again, thankfully. And now, her hat. She had loved that hat.

For months, she had been wearing that blue hat whenever she could. She'd wear it to school and hang it up in the coatroom and put it on after lunch and then, after recess, hang it up again always on the same hook. Not even her sister had a hat like that. No one did. It was a little too big for her with a flat brim that she felt hidden by.

Then one Tuesday near the end of the school year, it blew off her head. She ran and ran, but it blew over the fence where she was not allowed to go. She stopped running and watched it drifting away.

Goodbye, hat, she said to herself.

When recess was over and the class came back in and jackets and toys were put away and bodies were back in desks in their rows, the teacher was standing in front, holding something.

There it was, returned, her blue hat.

"Anyone recognize this?" the teacher asked, waving it like a magic wand. "Anyone?" she said. "Who belongs to this hat?"

Evangeline thought that was a strange way of asking the question. But she said nothing, curious to see who else would.

"No one?" the teacher said.

No one.

Evangeline knew that she was not invisible. But watching her hat hover up there without her in it, hearing nothing as nobody recognized it as hers, she felt that she was.

The teacher brought the hat to the office and there it remained, at the very top of the lost and found. She saw it in the mornings but couldn't bring herself to claim it. It didn't feel like hers anymore. She couldn't explain it. It was like, she hadn't lost the hat; the hat had lost her.

And did the hat miss her? It was silly, she knew, but she couldn't help wishing it did.

July

THE METAL OF THE bench is cold against their backs as Tess reads from the last list she'll read to Evangeline.

"Here we go," she says, "Astounding Animal Facts."

Tess reads: "Hippo milk is pink."

She reads: "'People with lactose intolerance can drink camel milk and feel fine.' Why is that, you think?" she asks.

"How should I know?" Evangeline says. "I just learned about it one second ago."

Tess nods.

"Are all these facts about milk?" Evangeline asks.

"No." Tess scans. "Just a few."

Why was that? Tess wonders. Who knows anymore? If Tess does not know, then no one knows. And no one will know.

She reads: "A blue whale has a heart so big that a person could swim through its valves."

Evangeline is quiet at that one, letting it crash over her. She can feel the empty space between her feet and the grass. A space that will not be there forever, but it is there now. She feels it like a solid thing pressing up on her body. It could grow right through her, she thinks. She is not scared of this emptiness, which is more real than she is but which also belongs to her.

Tess reads: "There are more fake flamingos than real flamingos by an order of magnitude."

Evangeline gives a rare smile. She says, "That could be true about people too," which is something Tess might say.

Tess studies her. She shakes her head, good-naturedly. "How can a person be both a child and a misanthrope?"

Evangeline does not know what that means and does not want to ask, so she imitates Tess again. "What is that," she says, "the start of a joke?"

In six days, Evangeline will be sent away with one box and one backpack to live with a grandfather she hardly knows. She will sleep in a small guest bedroom in his carpeted house that smells of rusted pennies and vitamins until she feels she is old but is only eighteen.

After that, she will visit her grandfather twice a year. She will not visit her sister or her father at her childhood home again. And yet, she will wake in a panic once a month on moonless nights, having forgotten, in her sleep, that the silence that roused her means nothing. That she is in a place now too far to hear the beeping machines.

One day, she will start to keep lists of her own, but she will never excel at it and will quickly abandon the endeavor. She'll write one list of questions, which is really a letter, and she will send it to her father.

Whenever she looks up at a red sunset, she will think of space and gamma rays bursting. She will not know that the woman has died, though she will suspect it. She will not know that the woman is buried in the cemetery where they met, in the plot right beside her own mother's grave. She will not go back to visit her mother or take any more grave rubbings of the headstone. And though the woman's name will be inscribed right beside it, in all those hours on all these Sundays they've spent together, they have never learned the other's real name.

As days pass into weeks and months and years, her own face will change so that it no longer looks like her memory of her sister's face. She will get a new hat, which is not blue, but which she will like even more than she liked the blue hat. She will forget about the first hat's blueness. In her memory, the hat will be black. Then she will forget the blue hat entirely. The longer she is not a ghost, the more she will forget what being a ghost felt like. The longer she stays outside the cemetery, the more she will forget what she had felt like therein.

And in four days, Tess will leave on a final long trip with her husband.

When she woke from her surgery, she found she hated him.

"I'm the one who is dying, you know," she wanted to scream but did not scream or even say quietly. Instead she wrote up a long list of things they might still see and do together. She tore it out of the notebook. They will be setting off to do and see the last of these things now.

Her husband will take photograph after photograph of her alone, as if he were not even with her on this journey, which in a sense—he is not. At first, each time he clicks the camera or crosses items off the list, the woman will want him to thank her, and when he does not thank her, she will want to tell him, "This is a gift I am giving you. All these memories."

A day will come toward the end of the list when she will find that she loves him again. It will feel different, her love, but not brand new. It will come back to her like she has rubbed the smudge marks off her glasses and put the glasses back on to see that, oh yes, they had some smudge marks before, but now they are clear.

She will write one more list before dying. Really, it is more of a poem. It's a list about time. She'd been thinking so much about it. How much time there is but how little is ours. She will memorize this list and repeat it in her head at the end. She will have said goodbye to everyone she could say goodbye to. She will think of the little girl and her bicycle. She will kiss her husband. She will think: We disappear so many times before we do, finally, disappear.

She will miss being a Martian. It seems unlikely, but she will hope she can be a Martian again.

BEFORE ALL THAT, WHICH is now, the sun has not yet set on the cemetery hills on a warm summer day. Tess and Evangeline have a bit more time to feel like a Martian and a ghost together. Evangeline will leave on Saturday and Tess on Thursday.

These minutes that are passing are their very last minutes. This bench they are sitting on is both the first and last bench.

-22-

After

THE WIND DELIGHTS HIM.

He loves the thrum of it in his ears, how it makes his eyes water. His beard is long and white but with the wind blowing through it, he feels young.

When he sails beyond the busy harbor, he likes to call out the way he did as a boy to get his grandmother's attention.

"Look at me, Gran!"

And though Adina is gone, he sees her in his mind's eye: rising from her flower beds, dusting off her gardening gloves, smiling at him under her visor.

"I am," she'd say. "I'm looking right at you."

He whoops with his head tilted back, letting the sea salt sting his throat. He must look a little crazy, he thinks. But he isn't crazy, just happy.

Ten years ago, the quake took everything in a matter of minutes.

It was months and months before the last bit of rubble was cleared, the caves filled in. The girl and her father could not be recovered. Three months later, Sylvia passed on the same day the insurance check arrived with its modest sum.

He'd already decided what he would do with the money.

The boat was a small, cheap fishing vessel. It had been advertised as "gently used." He did a cursory inspection. He knew almost nothing of boats, but he could tell that the hull was damaged below the waterline, that the wood was slightly corroded.

"I'll take it," he said anyway.

There was something he needed to see.

He bought a life jacket and after three lessons, he took the boat out on his own.

The lines kept tangling. He nearly capsized. The harbormaster had to come and arrange to have him towed back in.

So he wasn't able to see it that time.

He laughs to remember this. He has come to feel more himself—most himself—when at sea. He misses Sylvia. He'd have liked to show her that he didn't mind it anymore, the enormity of the wide-open ocean.

After that failed attempt, he took a few more lessons, tried again. The waters were calmer, so he did it at last: sailed far enough out to look back at Grace Beach.

It was a view he'd never had.

There it is, he thought, ancient Marks Island. The site of all his family history and personal tragedy. All that he'd ever tried and failed to make of his life.

Didn't it look beautiful without his museum perched on it?

He was surprised to think so.

He watched the sun set behind the ancient land. The pink sky had a texture like velvet.

"The past is gone," his grandmother used to say. "Why try to claim it?"

He likes to fish. There is a presence of mind to it that refreshes him. Sometimes, he'll see little fish on the surface of the water and he'll think of whales, so large, yet surviving off krill.

A line from the old litany will come back to him: *Time occurs at varying sizes and scopes.*

When the weather allows, he'll go farther out. There are more fish to catch. Plus, he likes to watch ancient Marks Island shrinking with distance until the whole stretch of land is a dot.

We are so small, he thinks, on the scale of almost anything. He's had this thought many times, but it's taken him all his life to come to embrace it.

"I remember you," the woman said.

This was right after the quake.

He'd gone out there—boatless and fully clothed in that raging ocean. The need to see it had overtaken him. The sky was golden and his museum was crumbling into the earth itself. The tallest waves he'd ever seen were cresting and he'd been trying to look back at his life without him in it when this woman had seen him, stopped him, saved him.

She pulled him back to shore, and it felt like a cosmic revelation: waking up to hear that he existed in someone else's memory. It was all that one could hope for.

When he bought the boat, it was unnamed. Or rather, every trace of its old name had peeled off. He planned to name it. He filled a few pages with a long list of options. But none of the new names he came up with felt right. In the end, he crossed them all out.

Some things, he's learned, can remain nameless.

Acknowledgments

THANK YOU TO ALEXA STARK FOR HELPING SHEPHERD this book from its earliest iteration into its final form. Thank you to Masie Cochran for believing in this novel, in its characters, and in me. Thank you to Craig Popelars, Nanci McCloskey, Beth Steidle, Alyssa Ogi, Elizabeth DeMeo, Becky Kraemer, Anne Horowitz, Allison Dubinsky, Jae Nichelle, Alice Yang, and the entire Tin House team, for your tremendous support. Thank you to Kate Bernheimer, Samantha Hunt, Allegra Hyde, and Tiffany Tsao, for reading with such great care.

I am endlessly grateful for the mentors and communities that sustained me during the years it took to bring this book into the world. It would not exist without each of you. Thank you.

To my brilliant workshop: Riley Cross, Travis Price, Marie Seegmiller, Cadwell Turnbull. To Diane Williams and the editors of *NOON*. To Rita Bullwinkel, Valerie Hsiung, Hilary Leichter, and Mary South. To Emma Komlos-Hrobsky for first bringing me to Tin House. Teachers: Joanna Defeo, Adrianne Harun, Joanna Howard, Josh Lambert, Helen Schulman, Darcey Steinke, Tiphanie Yanique. To my friends at the New School—especially my thesis cohort—and at Brown University. Thank you to the Sewanee Writers' Conference, Tent, and Art Farm.

To the kind friends who asked and listened, sent book recommendations and poetry newsletters, came to readings, provided distractions, and buoyed me when I needed it.

To my family: Mom and Dad, thank you for a childhood rich with stories, magic, and love. To my sisters, Jenna and Abby, my first and best friends. To Beth, Merle, Joe, Kinley, Harper, and Madison. To Janet, Neil, Michael, and Emily. To Lyla, Koshka, Tiger, and Topaz.

Grandparents: Pola Bergman, Wolf Bergman, Abraham Breitborde, Sylvia Breitborde, Lauretta Wolf. I miss you. I am grateful to remember you.

Thank you, Speedy, for making me less afraid.

Thank you, Penina, for making the whole world new.

And finally and forever, thank you, Andrew, for making ten thousand meals that have nourished my soul and for making every day lighter and utterly full.

© Phoebe Neel

REBEKAH BERGMAN's fiction has been published in *Joyland*, *Tin House*, *The Masters Review* anthology, and other journals. She lives in Rhode Island with her family.